The Wedding Pact A Collection of Christian and Amish Romance

Sylvia Davidson

Published by Trellis Publishing, 2021.

THE WEDDING PACT A COLLECTION OF CHRISTIAN AND AMISH ROMANCE

First edition. June 28, 2021.

Copyright © 2021 Sylvia Davidson.

ISBN: 979-8224163144

Written by Sylvia Davidson.

THE WEDDING PACT
SYLVIA DAVIDSON

THE WEDDING PACT

Chapter 1

"Are you following me?"

It probably came out sounding more like an accusation than a question, but Brooke Coleman was still reeling from discovering her least favorite person in the world, Derek Hodges, sitting in her office chair, with his Armani-clad feet propped up on her desk.

"You'd like that, wouldn't you?" he replied with a wink.

Brooke dropped her briefcase and purse in one of the leather chairs situated opposite from her desk and crossed her arms defiantly over her chest. It would've been so easy to let herself get distracted over the way he commanded the room with his very presence or the suggestive way his blue eyes roamed over her body as soon as she walked in the room. But, no, she wasn't going to let that happen. Not with Derek. Not *ever* with Derek Hodges.

"I thought I was through dealing with you for a little while now that the Ericson wedding is over," she remarked. "To what do I owe this honor?"

He threw his head back and laughed. If she wasn't so annoyed over his unexpected visit, Brooke would've let the deep, throaty sound of his laughter sink into her bones. Instead, she squared her shoulders and brushed it off without a second thought.

"It looks like you and I are going to be spending some more time together over the next few weeks. Your clients, Megan and Wade, contacted me late last night. They want to hire me as the event planner for their wedding. They've decided to have the ceremony at the Riverdale Cathedral and the reception at the Drake Hotel."

Brooke was livid. Honestly, she was beyond livid. At the moment, she couldn't even think of another word to describe just how angry she felt.

"*What?*" she exclaimed. "But we've been planning an outdoor wedding and reception at his father's lake house for two months now!"

Derek rose from behind the desk and stuffed his hands inside his pants pockets. He approached her cautiously, as if expecting her to pounce.

"Look, don't shoot the messenger. Megan said she would call you this morning when you got to work, and I just felt I should warn you first. After all, I know how much you love having me around."

He leaned in to her slightly, and the masculine scent of his cologne wafted through her senses and left her knees wobbly. For a moment, she thought he might kiss her, which was both exciting and ludicrous at the same time. After all, the man couldn't stand her, and the feeling was mutual.

The sound of her desk phone ringing snapped her back to reality.

"That's probably her right now. Do you want me to sit in on this one with you?" he asked.

He said it in his usual mocking tone, which made her temper bristle even more. Straightening her spine, Brooke placed her hands on her hips and glared at him.

"Slither back to your hole, Hodges."

Derek's shoulders slumped as he playfully pouted his lips.

"Now, Brooke...why do always have to say such hateful things to me? I'm crushed."

Before she could stop herself, Brooke lunged at him, flexing her hands and preparing to strike if he didn't move out of her way, which he did...and quickly. As she rounded her desk to answer the phone, Derek walked to the door, but not before flashing her another one of his winning smiles.

"I'm looking forward to working with you again, Brooke!"

Brooke snatched the cordless phone of its cradle just as the door closed behind him. If the closest heavy object hadn't been the expensive Tiffany paperweight she received from one of her favorite clients, she would've been tempted to hurl it at the door. Closing her eyes, Brooke inhaled deeply before putting the phone to her ear and attempting to carry on a civilized conversation.

This wedding couldn't be over with fast enough.

* * * *

Derek watched the scene unfolding before him, and he tried not to laugh – honestly, he did – but he knew without a doubt in his mind what was about to happen because he'd witnessed it many times before. Brooke Coleman was on the verge of snapping. Her beautiful green eyes darted back and forth between their clients, Megan and Wade, as if waiting for one of them to tell her the past few hours had been just a cruel joke.

"I'm so sorry, Brooke. I realize how hard you've been working on this wedding, and I know Wade had his heart set on us getting married at his parents' house, but the more I thought about it, the more I realized I wouldn't be able to live with myself if I didn't get married in my home church. It just wouldn't feel right."

Their voices echoed in the enormous cathedral sanctuary, even from the back row where Derek sat keeping his distance until the fireworks were over. Fortunately, the church was empty except for the four of them and the pastor, who flitted back and forth between the sanctuary and his adjoining office.

"And you're sure you want to have your reception at the Drake Hotel...on the other side of town?" Brooke inquired.

The couple glanced at each other, both looking apprehensive and unsure how to reply, but Brooke kept her composure. His gaze slid from her face to her long brown hair, which cascaded in soft waves over her shoulders and down her back. When she gently moved a strand of it away from her face and tucked it behind her right ear, he felt as if he'd been kicked in the gut.

If only she didn't despise him so much. True, it didn't help matters the way he always joked around with her, but he did it just to keep from tripping over his own tongue. She made the butterflies flip-flop inside his stomach whenever she was near, and she was the only reason he agreed to work for Megan and Wade in the first place. Otherwise, he would've told the wishy-washy couple to hit the road.

"I understand how you feel about having the ceremony here, Megan, but I just don't think you realize how difficult it's going to be trying to get everyone from the church to the hotel in time for the reception, especially here in the middle of town at five o'clock on a Friday afternoon. Can't you have the reception in the church dining hall?"

Wade shook his head.

"We thought about that, but the space isn't big enough. I suppose, if we needed to, we could try and whittle down the guest list."

Oh no…not another change.

That was his cue. Derek left his pew and walked down the aisle to stand beside Brooke, who was now fidgeting with the rings on her fingers while rocking back and forth on the tips of her toes. When he placed a hand against the small of her back, she jumped.

"If you don't mind, I've got to steal Brooke away for just a minute. We'll be right back."

Megan and Wade nodded as he led Brooke a few feet away where they wouldn't be overheard.

"Take a deep breath," he said. "You need to calm down."

Brooke jerked away from him.

"What on earth are you talking about? There's nothing wrong with me."

He motioned toward her hands and feet.

"I've worked with you enough times to recognize some of your quirks. You're twiddling your rings and doing that weird thing with your toes. You're also breaking out in hives around your neck. It happens every time you get mad."

Brooke rolled her eyes heavenward, but when she ran her fingertips over the welts on her neck, her eyes widened in fear for just a moment before she crossed her arms over her chest.

"Stop being ridiculous," she replied. "If that was the case I'd be covered from head to toes in hives every time I talked to you."

If she didn't look so cute and vulnerable, her comment probably would've stung, but now wasn't the time to get offended.

"Okay, you got me. Now, seriously, you need to get a grip. I know Megan and Wade are annoying, but we can get through this if we work together. Let them have their reception at the Drake Hotel, and I'll make sure everyone gets there on time. They don't need to start changing their guest list this close to the wedding."

She closed her eyes and took several deep breaths, and he waited patiently for her to speak, not wanting to break her concentration. Something he said must have gotten through to her because she stopped twitching, and it wasn't long before the redness around her throat began to slowly dissipate. His arms ached to hold her close and reassure her that everything would be okay, but he knew she wouldn't care for that...at least, not from him anyway.

"I'm sorry. I feel better now," she said. "Thank you, Derek."

She smiled at him then – a true, genuine smile – and it was so beautiful and so unexpected that it took his breath away. It was also the first time he could remember her calling him by his first name instead of Hodges.

"You're welcome. Now, let's get back over there before they decide to change something else."

She laughed.

"Good idea."

* * * *

The following six weeks flew by in a flurry of activity. Between dress fittings, a couple of florist fiasco's, the flower girl freaking out during rehearsal, and refereeing between Megan and Wade, Brooke was exhausted by the time their wedding day finally arrived. For a couple who'd supposedly been together eight years, the two of them sure couldn't agree on anything. Hopefully, they would be able to get through the ceremony and reception without arguing. Brooke was a tightly-wound bundle of nerves, and she took a couple of steady breaths to quell the anxiety wreaking havoc on her stomach.

Since she had spent most her time between the office and the church, and Derek worked on the venue at the hotel, they hadn't seen or talked to each other much, which was probably for the best. The last thing Brooke wanted or needed was more disagreements to add to the already growing list she'd acquired from the bride and groom.

Now the final countdown was on and in less than two short hours the wedding would be underway...hopefully. Brooke gave herself a quick once-over as she gazed into the bathroom mirror at the church. For someone who was run ragged, she had to admit she didn't look half bad, give or take some crow's feet around her eyes and lips that were in desperate need of some lipstick. She wondered what Derek would think of her new dress, but she dismissed the thought as quickly as it entered her mind. *Stop dreaming, Brooke.* After all, there really was no sense wasting time thinking about a relationship that would be doomed from the get-go.

"Brooke? Hello? Is this thing on?"

Brooke picked up her headset from the bathroom counter and fastened the microphone clip to her right ear before leaving the bathroom.

"I'm here, Denise. Everything okay? Did the florist drop off the arrangement for the foyer?"

With the bathroom downstairs near the fellowship hall, the transmission wasn't the best in the world, and Brooke had to strain her ears to understand her assistant over the crackle of static.

"Yes, it's here. The buses just arrived too."

Brooke stopped in her tracks.

"The what?" she asked.

She listened closely, but Denise's reply was inaudible because of the static, and Brooke rushed to the stairway so she could get to the entrance and find out what was going on. When she reached the top of the stairs, several wedding guests milled by on their way to the sanctuary and Brooke stopped to greet them with a smile and handshake.

The church foyer and sanctuary were packed to the brim with yellow roses and white daisies tucked in every nook and cranny imaginable. Of course, that decision hadn't come easily either, since Megan changed her color scheme three times before finally settling on yellow, pink, and white.

Brooke noticed a couple of the younger ushers were busy chatting on their cellphone's in a corner of the foyer. She snapped her fingers to get their attention, and within seconds the phones were turned off and they were standing at the sanctuary entrance, taking turns seating the steady stream of guests making their arrival.

"Denise? Where are you?"

There was a brief pause before Denise announced she was standing outside behind the church. Brooke furrowed a brow before walking quickly in that direction. Why in the world would she be outside, especially with the ceremony beginning so soon? When she turned the last corner of the hallway and made her way to the back door, she discovered her answer, and it wasn't at all what she expected. It was much, much worse.

Parked on the street behind the church were two larger than life charter buses. They were solid black with gold lettering and gold detailing on the front and sides, and from what she could tell by looking through the front windshield, the drivers were dressed in black suits with gold vests and bowties. The buses were huge and an eyesore – and that was putting it mildly. She felt the heat rise to her cheeks and her breath started coming in short gasps, but before she had the chance to explode her line of vision was suddenly skewed by big brown eyes and bouncy blonde curls.

"Now, Brooke, I know what you're thinking, but it's really not that bad."

Brooke shook her head profusely.

"Not bad? Are you kidding me, Denise? They look like strip clubs on wheels!"

Denise grasped Brooke's shoulders and spoke to her like she would a five-year-old, as if she was hoping it would keep her from throwing a temper tantrum. But Brooke was beyond pouting as this point. Derek showed up at that time, and when he brought his truck to a stop behind the buses, she pushed Denise to the side and headed straight for him.

He hopped out of his truck sporting a big grin on his face, and if Brooke hadn't been so upset, she probably would've spent more time admiring how handsome he looked in his suit and tie. His wavy black hair was combed back and neatly coifed, and she noticed he'd shaved off what little bit of facial hair he had since the last time she'd seen him. Any other time, her legs probably would've turned to rubber at the sight of him, but not this time.

"What were you thinking, Hodges?"

He looked behind him, as if he thought she might be shouting at someone else. A couple of people passing by on the sidewalk stopped to stare, but she couldn't care less. His long strides closed the distance between them in seconds, and when he placed a hand on her elbow and turned her around to walk back to the church, she jerked away from him.

"Hold on a second. What's the problem?" he asked.

She waved her hands in the air and gestured extravagantly toward the buses, but the confused expression on his face didn't change. He simply shrugged his shoulders, as if he couldn't fathom what the big deal was.

"*This* is what you came up with for transportation? Seriously?"

He rolled his eyes and laughed, and Brooke balled her fists by her side to keep from hitting him. His arrogance was infuriating, and she felt like kicking herself for trusting him.

"What did you think I was going to do, Brooke? Buy subway tokens for 200 people?"

Brooke threw her hands up and bit her bottom lip to keep from screaming. Leave it to Derek Hodges to do something like this to try and make her look bad in front of her clients and their guests. She should've known better. If she had just taken matters into her own hands, this wouldn't be happening.

Brooke turned abruptly on her heel and started walking toward the back door of the church.

"Brooke, wait!" he yelled.

Arguing with him was useless. Denise didn't try to stop her, but she'd worked as her assistant long enough to know better. With a quick glance at her watch, Brooke winced when she saw there was only an hour left until the wedding. Would there even be enough time to come up with some other mode of transportation? Somehow, she doubted it.

Brooke opened the door and slammed it behind her, causing the windows beside it to shake. Derek wasn't far behind. When he stormed through the door, she walked as fast as she could in the direction of the office. With any luck, the pastor wouldn't be there and she could use his phone in private.

A dozen scenarios played through her mind at once. Perhaps she could hire a limousine service to shuttle the guests back and forth between the church and hotel. She sighed. No, that would take too long, and they probably wouldn't on such short notice anyway.

"Brooke, would you wait a second!"

She kept walking.

"Brooke!"

Several of the guests were talking to each other in the corridor, and all of them stopped and looked when she rushed by. It didn't help that Derek kept calling her name either, since his deep voice kept bouncing off the walls in the narrow walkway.

One last turn and she would be home free. However, Derek was much quicker, and when he caught up to her and grabbed her by the arm, she had little time to respond before he started pulling her in the direction of what she knew to be a utility closet. For someone who seemed to always move at a turtle's pace, he was very agile, and within seconds he was shutting the door behind them and barring her from leaving.

"Let me go!" she yelled. "You're hurting me!"

Derek leaned over and flipped on the light switch. He wasn't *really* hurting her, but he didn't need to know that, and he did let go immediately, allowing her the opportunity to back away from him. The closet was small, and the dozen or so mops, brooms, and other cleaning supplies left little room for them to move around.

"Get out of my way, Hodges! Are you insane?"

Derek held up a hand to stop her from saying anything further.

"I had to do something. You were causing a scene out there."

Brooke rolled her eyes.

"*You* were the one yelling – not me."

Derek leaned over and grasped his knees. She could tell he was winded from chasing her, and it took him a few seconds before he could take a long, deep breath.

"For someone wearing stilettos, you sure can move."

Brooke stopped herself from smiling. She wasn't about to let her guard down. Not when she was still fuming over the whole bus fiasco.

"I should've known you would do something like this," she remarked.

Derek leaned back against the door.

"Like what?"

Brooke watched his expression, which never changed. There was no joking around, no grinning like a Cheshire cat, not even a playful wink. She shook her head in disbelief. He genuinely couldn't grasp why she was so upset.

"Like you hiring Hugh Hefner's convoy," she replied. "Did you not notice the tacky gold detailing and the drivers dressed like Blackjack dealers? Why are you trying so hard to make me look like a fool?"

Her comment made him laugh.

"Brooke? Everything okay?"

Brooked adjusted her earpiece, having totally forgotten she was wearing the headset and wondering how much Denise might have overheard.

"I'm fine, Denise. Please go upstairs and make sure Megan, Wade, and the bridesmaids and groomsmen are ready to get started. I'll be there shortly."

After Denise sent confirmation, Brooke turned off the transmitter clipped to her belt and removed the earpiece. Derek's gaze never wandered from her, and after a few moments of awkward silence, she was suddenly very aware of their close surroundings. The faint scent of his cologne lingered in the air, and Brooke swallowed hard past the huge lump that had formed in her throat.

"Why do you hate me, Brooke?"

He said it so softly she almost missed it, and his question surprised her. The mood in the room shifted instantly, and the playful glimmer in his gaze was replaced by something entirely different that bordered on sadness.

"I don't hate you," she replied. "Why would you think that?"

Derek stuffed his hands inside his pants pockets and shuffled his feet. For a moment, he didn't say anything, and Brooke braced herself for the worst.

"When I'm around, I never see you smile. You tense up as soon as I walk in a room. You might not notice it, but I do. I feel it."

He looked at her again, and the softness in his eyes made her stand up a little straighter. It was the first time she could recall them having a serious discussion that didn't involve bickering, and she honestly didn't know how to respond. It made her heart ache knowing he thought of her in such a way. What he viewed as contempt for him couldn't have been more opposite of how she truly felt.

"Derek..."

He took a step toward her and Brooke suddenly found herself caught between him and a tall stack of shelves loaded with cleaning supplies. There was no room to escape and barely enough space between them to breathe. When he reached out and touched her cheek, she thought for sure her heart had stopped beating.

"I promise I didn't rent those charter buses to try and make you look bad. I honestly thought I was doing something good...something that would help you worry a little bit less. I know you've had your hands full with Wade and Megan and this wedding. The only reason I even agreed to be their event planner was so I could be near you."

His confession made Brooke's heart thump erratically. It also made her feel horrible over the way she reacted.

"I'm sorry I overreacted. Having to deal with their constant arguing and the changes they've been making has almost gotten the best of me. The buses are fine. Really. If they don't like it, then I'll deal with it."

Derek shook his head.

"No. I will. You've dealt with enough already."

Brooke nuzzled her cheek against his palm.

"I've never hated you, Derek. I'm sorry if I've done anything to make you feel that way. It's just...whenever we're in the same room together, it seems like you're always trying to make me angry, and I don't understand why."

He looked down at her and smiled.

"It's not you, Brooke. It's me. I don't know how to act around you. I never have," he explained. "When I see you, my heart starts pounding, and I get tongue-tied. The only reason I joke around with you is so I won't say something stupid and make a fool out of myself. I honestly don't mean to make you mad."

She didn't know what to say. How could it be they'd worked together so many times over the years and she'd never caught on to his true feelings? Her heart ached for the time they'd wasted and could never get back.

Brooke grasped his hand and slid it down the side of her neck and over her chest, pausing it at her heart, which was now racing uncontrollably. The heat from his touch seared through the thin material of her dress and left her breathless. Perhaps it was time they were both completely honest with each other.

"Being near you has the same effect on me," she whispered.

He closed his eyes for a moment and when he opened them, the passion was evident in the way his eyes glistened as he gazed at her, sending a chill up her spine. It was the first time in many years Brooke could recall a man looking at her so tenderly, and she braced her back against the shelf to keep from sliding into a heap on the floor. She wanted to kiss him so badly, but she also didn't want to rush the moment. For the time being she was content just to stand close to him and enjoy the warmth of his touch as it seared her clothing and made her light-headed.

Derek moved his hand up and over her left shoulder. Ever so slowly he slid his fingertips down her arm, causing her to tremble. When he leaned in to her, she held her breath expectantly, but he didn't kiss her. Instead, he gently pressed his lips to her bare shoulder. It was the subtlest of moves, but the effect it had on her was more profound than she anticipated. He laced his fingers in her long hair and gently pulled her head back so her throat was exposed for his enjoyment.

Brooke closed her eyes and completely lost herself in the way each brush of his lips unraveled her bit by bit until she was left gripping the shelf behind her to keep from falling. He took his time and never rushed. It was an exquisite torture. In many ways, it was almost too much to bear, but in other ways it wasn't nearly enough. When she felt him back away, she was perfectly content to plead with him for more, if that's what it took.

"Derek…"

But pleading wouldn't be necessary. No sooner had his name left her lips when he was pulling her close and claiming her mouth with his own. Brooke wrapped her arms around his neck and clutched him as tightly to her body as humanly possible. His mouth was unrelenting, and every nerve in her body was on fire. She didn't want it to end. Brooke clung to him, and she reciprocated each kiss with the same urgency.

The sound of heavy footsteps in the hallway interrupted the stillness, making them pause. Brooke held her breath, half expecting the pastor or some other church official to throw open the door and catch them in their hiding spot. Although she knew it would probably be best if they stopped before they got caught, the thought of letting Derek go bothered her much more. He never loosened his grip on her, even as the footsteps grew louder and louder, until they stopped right outside the utility room door. Derek's mouth was very close to her ear, and as his warm breath slid over her skin, she did her best to remain perfectly still, which wasn't easy. Her heart felt as if it would pound right out of her chest – partly from fear but mostly from Derek standing so close.

She struggled to control her labored breathing for what felt like an eternity, until the person outside their door finally decided to walk on and continued down the hallway. The sound of their footsteps grew lighter and lighter until they disappeared completely and Brooke expelled the long, painful breath she'd been holding for far too long.

"That was close," Derek whispered.

The shelf she rested against began to dig into her skin, and Brooke grabbed the lapels on Derek's suit jacket and pushed him back against the door. It caused a loud thud, but he didn't seem to mind. If anything, her strength and determination seemed to surprise him. When he clutched the belt around her waist and pulled her to him, it didn't take long for them to pick up where they left off. The hardness of his body made her pulse quicken, and she barely had time to catch a breath between each kiss before he was crushing his lips to hers again and expertly drawing her in – closer and closer – until she was left trembling in his arms.

"Brooke!"

Startled, Derek and Brooke jumped apart as Denise's voice filled the tiny space around them. She could hear Denise's high-heels clicking against the marble floor as she walked the hallway, obviously searching for her, and Brooke panicked as she glanced at her watch. Only fifteen minutes until the wedding! Derek was already straightening his clothes and smoothing his hair into place. Unfortunately, there wasn't enough time left to run to the bathroom and check her appearance in the mirror, so she smoothed down the front of her dress and hoped for the best.

"Promise me we'll pick up where we left off once this wedding is finally over," he said.

Brooke leaned up on her tip-toes and kissed him.

"I promise."

Brooke opened the door just enough so she could peer outside. When the coast was clear, she opened it the rest of the way, nearly bumping into Denise, who was approaching from the opposite direction. Denise's jaw slacked open, and her gaze grew wide, but it didn't take long before she was grinning at them both. Brooke felt the heat rise to her cheeks, but there wasn't time to try and explain – not that she felt she owed an explanation. Seeing the two of them sneaking out of the utility closet probably said it all.

The three of them raced toward the sanctuary just as Megan and her bridesmaids descended the stairway. The plan was for Denise to stay behind and direct any guests that arrived late. Derek would linger nearby to help direct guests to the waiting charter buses as soon as the ceremony was over. Brooke closed the double-doors to the sanctuary and helped Megan and the rest of the bridal party find their appropriate spots in line.

She tried not to glance at Derek unless it was necessary, to keep from breaking her concentration, but every so often she would catch him staring at her, and she was reduced to a jittery puddle of nerves all over again. Knowing she would be in his arms again once the wedding was over didn't help matters either. The "I do's" couldn't come fast enough, as far as she was concerned.

Brooke looked over the line one last time. The bridesmaids were in place, the flower girl wasn't freaking out, but Megan was clutching her father's arm so tight she was worried she might break it.

"Everyone take a deep breath. It will all be over soon."

They laughed, and Megan expelled a long, deep breath, but her dad was very still and quiet. He appeared just as anxious, if not more so, than his daughter, so Brooke gave his arm an affectionate squeeze, which seemed to break the ice and brought a smile to his face.

Suddenly the air was filled with the sound of the pianist playing the Bridal March, and Brooke gave Derek a quick wink before grasping the knobs on the sanctuary doors.

"Here we go. Time to get this show on the road."

* * * *

Derek helped the hotel staff fold up the last remaining chairs in the reception hall and move them out of the way. Every so often he would glance across the room and catch himself watching Brooke like some lovelorn teenager.

It felt good.

She sat at one of the dinner tables with her feet now stiletto-free and propped up on a chair in front of her. It had been a very long night. The wedding had, thankfully, gone off without a hitch, but the reception lasted longer than anticipated, mainly because the alcohol kept flowing and the band kept playing. Now that everyone was gone, the enormous room seemed far too quiet.

While the hotel staff cleared tables and continued cleaning, Derek walked over to Brooke and extended his right hand. She looked up at him curiously.

"I don't believe I've had the privilege of dancing with you at any of the weddings we've worked on together," he remarked.

Brooke gazed around the room.

"That might be a little difficult now that the band is gone."

Derek grabbed her hand and pulled her to the center of the room, which only two hours prior was packed to overflowing with people of all ages dancing and having a good time. He had every intention of asking Brooke to dance during the reception, but unfortunately, he stayed busy the entire time tending to caterers and kitchen staff.

"I can hear the music," he replied. "Just use your imagination."

Derek wrapped his arms around her waist and held her close as they swayed together. Some of the hotel employees gave them quizzical glances as they walked by, but as far as he was concerned, he and Brooke were the only people in the room. She rested her head against his chest, and he breathed in the heady scent of her perfume.

"So, where do we go from here?" he asked.

She looked up at him and smiled.

"I'm not sure. What do you suggest?"

He couldn't resist the urge to kiss her any longer, and when he pressed his lips to hers for a brief moment, she closed her eyes and sighed.

"I think we should take a few days off work and go on an extended vacation so we can discuss the possibilities. I believe we've earned it," he said.

Brooke squeezed him tight before resting her head on his chest again.

"I couldn't agree with you more. Where should we go?

He grinned.

"It doesn't matter to me. If you're there, then I'm happy."

She didn't say anything, but she put her hands on his cheeks and stood on her tip-toes so she could place a tender kiss on his lips, which spoke more to his heart than words ever could. She felt so small and fragile in his arms, and he wished they could stay there in that very moment forever.

"You know, I bet if we combined our talents we would make an awesome team," he said.

Brooke stopped swaying to the "music" and took a took a step backward. She looked up at him curiously, and he worried he might have said the wrong thing, but when she started grinning, he breathed a little easier.

"You mean our jobs?" she asked.

He nodded.

"It was just a thought. If we combined your wedding planner skills and my event planner skills, we could have a very lucrative business. Besides, we work together so much already."

Brooke's gaze took on a faraway look, as if she might be considering it. After a few seconds, she rubbed her fingers against her chin and began to nod.

"We could call it B&D Enterprises or B&D Wedding Planners."

Her eyes began to sparkle, which excited him and also worried him a bit. There was no telling what was going on inside that beautiful mind of hers.

"Wait a minute. Why not D&B Enterprises or D&B Event Planners?" he asked.

Her lips puckered into a sour expression, which made him laugh, and he wrapped an arm around her waist as they began making their way back to the table.

"We can discuss it, but I think you'll end up agreeing with me that B&D has a better ring to it."

He laughed again.

"I guess that means we won't be able to date each other. You know what they say about dating a coworker...bad luck and all."

Brooke looked up at him and winked.

"I've never heard that. I've always been told dating someone you work with can be pretty exciting."

Derek pulled her close so he could whisper in her ear.

"If it gets any more exciting than it has already, I don't think my poor heart can take it."

She laughed at that, and the beautiful sound reached right inside his chest and squeezed hard. She slipped on her shoes while Derek put on his jacket, and together they left the hotel, hand in hand. He did know one thing for certain...he was anxious to get started.

THE TRAIN STATION

EMMA WRIGHT

21

The train screeched to a halt and Elaine Sheldon had to brace herself for the onslaught of people trying to squeeze past out. Holding tightly around the handrail, she winced when a rushing man bumped his laptop bag against her hips, and she took a few steps back with the impact.

The man did not stop to apologize and Elaine only heaved a sigh and fixed her stance as the train resumed moving.

It was supposed to be a five-minute walk from the station to her apartment, but tonight, it did not feel like it. Her steps were slow and her shoulders were drooped. The streetlights refused to turn on properly and it flickered repeatedly as she passed by. Elaine sighed at the dreary atmosphere.

Just a week ago, these walks home passed by with a spring in her step, looking forward to the person who was waiting for her to be back, the person she had been going home to for the past six months, the man who welcomed her with a warm hug and a big smile after a tiring day at work—until the other day.

Her eyes felt heavy and the long wait for the elevator was not helping with her mood. She watched as the red arrow went down as minutes passed by until it reached the ground floor. Her ride back up was spent alone. She smiled bitterly. The world must really hate her.

All doors were closed when she alighted at the twelfth floor except for one. For a second, she almost panicked thinking that the opened door was hers, only to realize that it was the empty unit beside hers. Boxes are stacked in front of the door and the sound of a man's groans can be heard as she came closer.

She battled with herself if she should help or not. As the next-door neighbor, she knew she should, as a sign of welcome for the new occupant, but she also knew that the feeling in her chest is heavier than those boxes. She scoffed at her dramatics but looked down at herself. Her arms were already crying in protest with her handbag and laptop bag and those boxes looked nowhere near light so she forgot being thoughtful for once and unlocked her door. She was about to go inside when a man's voice startled her.

"Hi. Do you live next door?" The man beamed at her but the smile didn't reach his eyes.

Elaine smiled back, a closed-lip one. "And you must be my new neighbor," she offered her hand which the man accepted. "Elaine."

"Ivan. It's nice to meet you," he let go of her hand and gestured at the boxes. "I'll be done in a minute. You don't have to worry about the noises." He smiled again but Elaine can only see a grimace.

"Don't worry, take your time. I would have helped you but—"

Ivan waved his hand no. "No need. You must be tired from work," he observed, noticing the formal attire and the laptop bag hanging on her shoulders. "Go on ahead. Have a good night."

"You too," she returned in a clip tone and sent a brief smile again before going inside. The bang of the door echoed throughout the dark empty unit, reminding Elaine that she had no company anymore, that she had to spend the night alone in her empty apartment.

A tear escaped down her cheeks, which ended with bouts of sobbing for the third consecutive night.

—-

There are things in life that once you get a taste of, you'd never want to let go. And for Elaine, that was her relationship with Christian.

They started dating a little over a year ago, when they met at a mutual friend's party, though neither are close enough to the celebrant and her friends so they ended up chatting the night away. A week later, they found themselves agreeing to date exclusively.

Elaine did not have high hopes with her relationship at the start. Christian seemed to be the happy go-lucky type of guy who always acted on a whim instead of having plans. She wasn't in too deep yet, so she didn't mind it at all.

But as the months go by and their relationship turned for the better, people around them started to notice—that Christian is changing for the good and it was mainly because of his relationship with Elaine. It flattered the female, she won't deny it. Knowing that she may be one of the reasons why Christian was trying to find a stable job, having the courage to pursue his passion in photography, and planning for his future, made her pleased.

All along, Elaine was expecting that she was included in the plan. It only dawned on her that she was never part of the picture when one day, she got home, expecting the smell of pepperoni and cheese for their usual pizza night, only to find a large bag filled with all of Christian's things that had accumulated in her home. They never agreed to stay together officially but they might as well be for all the days and weekends the male had stayed with her.

At first, she thought he was going for a vacation. She could've accepted it, a six-month out of the country trips to take images of the wonders of nature. What she didn't understand was why he had to break up with her.

They could've made it worked, Elaine believed so. She trusted herself to stay faithful and she put the same amount of trust on Christian. It just so happened that her ex-boyfriend did not believe in long distance relationships. It even hurt more when he said that he's not even sure if he's even coming back. His career was just starting, he said. It could be his one in a lifetime opportunity, he said. All Elaine could do was cry and beg him to at least try, but he was already decided.

And that was it. The end of a year-long relationship in just a snap.

—

The pastor was going through the sermon part and Elaine pinched her forearm to stay focused. They had to work overtime last night and she barely had a wink of sleep before she raced to be on time to the church.

Attending the mass was a weekly thing for Elaine. Christian never accompanied her no matter how much she forced him to and now, she's secretly grateful because at the least, she has this one activity she was used to doing alone.

The pastor's voice resounded against the walls and she snapped back into attention. Someone, a man perhaps judging by the black slacks and the scent, sat beside her. She almost rolled her eyes for the man's tardiness but bit her lips when she realized that she was no better for drifting off instead of listening.

The pastor droned on and she could hear the sound of the piano and the jingle of the tambourine but it faded as her lids became heavier.

By the time she woke up, people were standing up and were walking towards the exit. Elaine jolted in her seat, lifting her head from a sturdy shoulder she was leaning on, cheeks crimsoning due to the embarrassment.

She looked to her right and her eyes widened while the color of her cheeks got redder. "Ivan," she muttered. Of all people to fall asleep on while a mass was ongoing, it had to be her new next-door neighbor.

Ivan chuckled and raised his hand to his lip, which confused Elaine. When it dawned on her, she turned around and wiped the bit of drool that escaped her lips.

Clearing her throat and checking discreetly if there was still drool left, she turned back again to an amused Ivan. At least now, the smile reached his eyes unlike the first time she saw him.

"I'm sorry for falling asleep on you," she pursed her lips. An old lady passing by gave her a stink eye and she refused to shrink on her seat in shame.

Her neighbor saw the gesture and he chuckled. "It's okay. You went home late didn't you?"

"How did you know?" Her eyebrows furrow.

Ivan looked more amused now. "I heard your door. It wasn't exactly hard to when it's the dead hour of the morning," he explained.

Elaine nodded, laughing at herself for thinking of anomalous things such as Ivan being a stalker or a creep. It crossed her mind that it was still strange for him to be awake at such an hour but then that would mean it was also strange for her to have just come home so she didn't bring it up.

"Oh!" She unconsciously glanced over his shoulder and found a tiny, wet mark. Scrambling for tissues, she pulled a handful and wiped at his clothes furiously. "I am so sorry," she apologized repeatedly until Ivan had to hold her hand to stop her.

"It's spit. No big deal. No one's gonna die," he smiled once again. Elaine thought he should smile more often. It brightens up his face. Meanwhile, her face was on fire.

"Can I treat you for coffee then? As sorry and welcome?"

"I'd love to but I have somewhere to be. Maybe next time," he said noncommittally.

"Next time then." She apologized again before racing back home. A loud 'I'm home' is on the tip of her tongue but she stopped herself just in time.

Elaine dragged her feet to the sofa and flopped down unceremoniously with her legs hanging on an arm. Tears cascaded down her temples, which progressed into sobs. Her chest felt tight and her breath was constricted.

Earlier, she prayed to God to give her Christian back. She wished that Christian would change his mind and call her, or at least send her a message, saying sorry and that he wants her back.

She was praying but the pain hurt like hell. She asked God why did this have to happen to her, why she had to feel such pain, why she had to feel hopeful for her future for once, only for it to crumble right in front of her.

It was so unfair. She gave it her all but all she got was nothing.

—-

It had been a month since the breakup and Elaine was faring better. She haven't cried herself to sleep for two weeks now and she even had the energy to go out for a walk. It wasn't much but it was a start. She still thought of her ex-boyfriend from time to time, which was inevitable considering every corner of her apartment reminded her of him, but the pangs were getting less painful. In a way she didn't know how, she was getting by.

It was a Sunday and she was on her way to the church. A friend, Leslie, welcomed her with a hug.

"You're looking great, dear." The shorter female brushed her cheek against Elaine's and Elaine had to chuckle at her affections.

"Hi, how have you been? I haven't seen you here lately?"

Leslie beamed at her in delight. "I went on a vacation with Luis to France. Oh, we have to get some coffee later. I have lots of stories to tell you," she narrated giddily, the smile never wavering off her face.

"How's Christian? Still sleeping I bet?" Leslie chuckled and Elaine's eyes twitched. She swallowed a lump in her throat and an awkward silence passed before her friend realized that something was wrong.

"Hey, what's wrong?"

Elaine cleared her throat and forced a smile. "W-we broke up," she cursed at herself for stuttering. It felt more real every time she had to say it outloud and it doubled the sharp pain that coursed through her.

Leslie looked shocked beyond belief at the news and scrambled to wrap her arms around Elaine again. "I'm so sorry!"

Elaine, who had to fight the tears that were threatening to come out, hugged her back, glad to have someone to comfort her even if it was a month late. "It's okay. It's been a month."

She pulled back and wiped the tears that escaped despite her resistance. "I'm all right," she forced out a smile. Her friend looked at her worriedly but let it go for now. "All right, let's have lunch together okay?" Leslie asked, to which Elaine said yes. It had been a while since she had a meal with another person aside from her co-workers and she welcomed the thought now more than ever.

The mass lasted for a little over an hour and Leslie pulled her to a nearby Italian cafe that served great pasta and gelato. Elaine was grateful for the distraction but she could not help but glance at a table for two at a corner. She mentally sighed and erased the memories in her head.

—-

Elaine was working on a report when a call came. Not expecting anybody, she looked at her phone quizzically, which registered Leslie's name. Leslie rarely contacted her through the phone.

Surprised, she accepted the call and had to brace herself for a joyful Leslie who almost screeched a 'hello.'

"Hey, what's up?" Elaine reclined back on her seat and shut her eyes. She could hear her stomach grumbling only to remember that she didn't eat anything for lunch.

"I know this might be too soon, but it's been two months and it's not too soon right?" She said rapidly and Elaine had to sit up straight again and focus on her words to keep up.

"What exactly might be too soon?"

Leslie paused dramatically. Elaine could almost hear her excitement through the receiver.

"Dating."

"Dating?" Elaine repeated dumbly.

"Yeah, dating. I figure it's about time you meet new people. What do you think?" Elaine processed everything before saying an alarmed 'what' as a reaction.

She sighed before continuing. "Leslie, I know you have the best intentions in mind. But if you still didn't know, I barely have time to meet new people."

"But you have the time," Leslie insisted. "Every Sundays. Don't you always save your Sundays?"

"I do. But that's for church and some me time. I don't feel like going to a party or anything after a mass."

"Exactly. For church. And forget the me time, you have more than enough of that," Leslie paused and apologized for the insensitive remark, which Elaine only waved away. Leslie was just telling the truth.

"What I actually wanted to say is that I know this guy, from the church we go to, who you might be interested to meet," Leslie drawled on. It took a minute before it registered what she was suggesting.

"Are you setting me up on a blind date?" She asked incredulously.

"Uh, yes," her friend admitted sheepishly.

Elaine rubbed a thumb on a temple. "Do I have a say on this?"

"Not really. I already set up the time and date."

"Leslie—!"

"I had to! I know you're gonna say no!"

"Whatever. Just text me the details. I have work to do," Elaine grumbled. She heard a faint 'I love you' before she hung up the phone and she felt a little bad for not saying it back to her dear friend.

—-

That night, Elaine turned and tossed on her bed. She couldn't stop thinking about the blind date and she had bombarded herself with too much questions that only left her more confused and doubtful.

Is it too soon? What if Christian knows about it? What if the guy isn't what she's expecting him to be? But then, what exactly are her expectations?

The fact that he goes to her church is a good point, but the thought that she saw it as a good point gnaws at her guilt. It might be ridiculous but she felt guilty for indirectly saying yes to the blind date. It had been two months but thinking of a possibility of a relationship with anyone other than Christian brought a bad taste to her mouth.

—-

Elaine pushed the glass door open before a waitress assisted her to her seat. A man was already seated at the table, but she could not see his face yet.

A gasp escaped her lips when the waitress stopped and gestured at their table, making the man look up.

"Elaine?" Ivan said, sounding shell-shocked himself.

"You're Leslie's friend?" Elaine asked for good measure. She had not seen her neighbor for weeks now. The last time, they only exchanged brief hellos when they happened to meet while taking out trash.

Ivan stood up and helped her pull her seat back, before returning to his own side.

"And you are Leslie's friend," Ivan jokingly deadpanned. Elaine took her seat and began to chuckle. Ivan, amused by the situation, also began to laugh.

"I guess we'll be having a date today?" He asked with a smile on his face. Elaine hummed in affirmation while smiling from ear to ear.

"How did you meet Leslie?" Elaine asked once their food was served.

"I actually knew Luis first. He was an old friend and he was the one who suggested this place for me to move to," Ivan explained before taking a bite of the grilled chicken.

Elaine took a sip of water before responding. "Why did you move? Was it for your job?"

The question froze Ivan for a second before he relaxed. Elaine bit her tongue for the question which obviously hit a nerve.

"You don't have to answer it if you don't want to," She said softly.

"Sorry," he offered a timid smile.

"It's okay," she smiled before diverting the conversation to a different topic.

It turned out that they have a lot of similar interests than they could have expected. They have the same fascination with the Harry Potter series, the same geeky side when it came to Star Wars, and the same passion when it came to football—though Elaine loved Man U with a passion while Ivan preferred Chelsea.

Hours later, they found themselves laughing comfortably around each other while they walk together home. They stopped when they reached Elaine's door and Ivan kept a good distance, to which Elaine was grateful for.

"I really had a lot of fun," Ivan smiled.

"Me too. I think it's been ages since I've laughed that much," Elaine gushed.

He put his hands in his pant's back pockets and Elaine mentally chuckled.

"We should do this again some other time?" It was more of a question rather than a statement.

Elaine let out a deep breath she didn't know she had been holding and nodded. "Sure."

—-

She threw the frame inside the black plastic bag and flinched at the sound of breaking glass. Next were the t-shirts and boxers that were definitely not hers, followed by other toilet utilities that were never meant for a woman.

It was a day after her blind date and last night, she had the urge to throw away everything that reminded her of Christian. It had been months but she still kept some of his belongings that he left there, silently holding on to the hope that he would come back.

This move did not mean anything but a sign of her trying to move on. She had been meaning to do it for weeks but the date with Ivan was the last push she needed to start working on it. She sniffed and sobbed for the first few minutes but it got better as the plastic bag got fuller.

It was filled with pictures, letters, dried flowers, candy and chocolate wrappers, and almost every single thing that Christian gave her during their relationship, including the bracelet that he gifted to her last Christmas. It took a lot of emotional effort but afterwards, she felt lighter, as if an invisible baggage was thrown away.

The door next to her opened just as she was pulling the plastic bag outside to throw it in the bin. Ivan looked as surprised as she was. He was sporting a shirt paired with loose shorts and running shoes.

"Going for a run at night?" She asked, eyeing his outfit.

Ivan shrugged. "The park's good enough for some laps."

Elaine stopped for a second to think before taking a leap of faith. "Mind if I join you?"

—

The night was a bit chilly but fortunately, there was minimal wind.

Elaine had been living in that neighborhood for years but it was the first time that she jogged at the park. She always thought it was full of rowdy teenagers getting drunk or creeps who had nothing better to do with their lives. Ivan laughed at her when she voiced it out.

"This place's actually good," He panted, arms swinging as they jogged around the vicinity. "You should just avoid Friday nights because it can be too crowded."

She looked at him curiously. "How long have you been going here?" She asked, breaths coming short. Ivan slowed his pace a bit.

"Since the first week I moved," he answers. "It was a bit lonely staying indoors."

Elaine stopped in her tracks, causing Ivan to stop too.

"I am so sorry for being a very unwelcoming neighbor. I should have made you something and came over to check on you."

Ivan rested a hand on her head and ruffled her hair. Elaine felt like pulling away but didn't, surprised at how large his hand felt. "No need to feel sorry. I know it wasn't your best day then," he continued jogging and she followed automatically.

She gulped as she remembered that day. It was definitely one of her most miserable days. "Yeah. My boyfriend just broke up with me a few days before that," she chuckled dryly. This time, it was Ivan who stopped first.

"I am so sorry to hear that."

She pursed her lips in thought. "It's okay. I've been doing great. It wasn't an excuse to not welcome you," she patted his shoulder, signaling him to continue moving.

It was silent for a few minutes before Ivan spoke up again.

"I just got divorced a few months ago."

Elaine screeched to a halt. "What?" Her eyes widen at her rude reaction. "I mean, when?"

"A few weeks before I moved," Ivan looked down. "My ex-wife and I just got divorced and I realized I can't stay at our home for long so I sold it, and moved here," he gestured at his surroundings with feigned enthusiasm. "And I think I made a great decision."

Elaine took a step closer before wrapping her arms around him. "I am sorry to hear that."

She could feel him shaking his head as he hugged her back. "I guess we're both sorry to hear about each other's heartbreaks?" he joked to lighten the mood. She pushed him back and hit him lightly on the chest before laughing.

They both broke into fits of laughter, earning the questioning looks of the passers-by.

—

They continued to contact each other throughout the week. They may be neighbors but Elaine frequently opted to work until late night so they can't really meet much. Leslie called once to check on how the date went and squealed when Elaine responded with a simple 'Thank you' and shouted 'I knew it, I knew it' repeatedly until it burned Elaine's ears.

The following Sunday, Elaine and Ivan agreed to go to the church together, causing Leslie to get excited upon seeing them.

She looked at them knowingly and winked at Elaine, who blushed at her friend's action. Ivan chuckled at the sight but pretended that he did not see it. All of them, including Luis, Leslie's boyfriend, sat side-by-side inside the church.

During the mass, Elaine prayed and asked for guidance, if what she was doing was right or if it was too soon to consider liking a different man. When she opened her eyes and looked at Ivan's direction, she found him to be staring back at her.

She glanced away and fought down the blush that crept on her cheeks.

—

It was a Wednesday night and usually, Elaine would still be at work, doing things that were not really urgent.

When she got home, it was way too early for bedtime and she found herself thinking of the man living in the unit beside hers. Curiously, she laid an ear flat on the surface of the wall to check for any noises. She didn't know why but she wanted to check if Ivan was home.

She could hear a faint sound of music and she thought about it once, twice, and multiple times before deciding to send him a message.

A few minutes later, there were knocks on her door. Elaine, already clad in more comfortable clothes, welcomed the sight of Ivan carrying chips and soda.

"Did you bring any DVDs?" She helped him bring the things to her living room and settled them on the coffee table. Ivan reached for his back and pulled out some cases and handed them to her.

She raised her eyebrows at the choices. "So you're basically suggesting we watch the whole series of Harry Potter?" She looked at him pointedly.

Ivan shrugged before making himself comfortable on the couch. "Pretty much," he grinned.

In the middle of the movie, they found themselves sitting close to each other, shoulders almost bumping. Elaine looked at her side and it was only a few inches away from Ivan's. Unconsciously, she continued to stare until he looked back.

"Like what you see?" he grinned mischievously, earning a smack on his chest.

"Your scar," she started, pertaining to a small scar at the left corner of his lips.

"Ah, they're battle scars," he jested. Her forehead scrunched at the vague answer.

Ivan sighed before reclining fully. "I had a bit of a scuffle last year. I saw my then wife with another man and I confronted them right on the spot. And the rest is history," he smiled but the bitterness was pronounced.

Elaine copied his position and leaned her head on his shoulder. It was a bold move and she was holding her breath if the male would shrug her off. However, Ivan lifted his arm and rested it on her shoulder so she could scoop closer. Elaine let the tension seep out of her body.

"I only have one question," she said after a while.

"What is it?" He closed his eyes, hoping that he could answer it whatever the question was.

"He got it worse right? I mean, you managed to hit his face at least twice? With bruises?"

Ivan burst out laughing. "Yes, yes, I did. I kicked him in the stomach, too. It was pretty satisfying," he answered, still chuckling at the unexpected question.

"Good," She said before placing an arm over his stomach.

They watched the rest of the movies in the same position.

—-

Elaine was typing her report when her boss approached her.

"I read your latest report, about the success rate if the company decides to venture in e-commerce." She waited with bated breath. It was a report she had been working extra hard for.

"And I can say I'm impressed. I sent a copy to the higher-ups and we just have to wait for their comments," he patted her on the shoulder.

Elaine beamed and said thank you.

"You should continue doing what you've been doing recently," he commented, puzzling Elaine.

"I mean, you look happier. Whatever the reason is, continue doing it," he said before turning back to his office.

Elaine could only think of one big change in her life recently. Biting her lips to stop herself from grinning too widely, she smiled at the thought of a man.

—

She was preparing the TV and the player for their usual movie night when Ivan received a call. His expression dimmed and his jaw locked when he saw who was calling but still answered it, walking towards the kitchen for some privacy.

Elaine, though worried, stayed where she was and fiddled with her own phone. She tried to give Ivan the privacy he needed but was surprised when his voice got louder.

"I don't give a fuck about it. I'm deleting your number. Please don't call me anymore."

She could hear the sound of a phone hitting the floor and she scrambled off the sofa to check on him.

Ivan was staring at the broken device and his chest was heaving deeply. Slowly, she walked towards him and reached for his shoulders. He relaxed at the touch and rubbed a hand on his face.

"I'm sorry you have to hear that," he reached for her hand and pulled her closer to him before hugging her waist.

Elaine put her hand on his hair and carded her fingers through the black strands.

"It was my ex-wife," he explained, making Elaine halt her actions for a moment. She only resumed when Ivan nudged her hand with his head. "She was telling me about her wedding in two weeks, and that I'm invited." He laughed bitterly. "She cheated on me and she had the guts to invite me to her wedding."

Elaine, now shaken, fought the tears that are threatening to spill. She can feel the hurt from Ivan's voice and it was affecting her more than it should.

She remained silent, listening to Ivan's breath until he completely relaxed and his breaths evened out.

The silence was deafening until Elaine had the courage to break it. "Do you still love her?"

It was a yes-no question but Ivan didn't respond for the next two seconds, nor even for the next minutes.

Feeling defeated, Elaine pulled herself from his grasp, ignoring his pleas to make her stay. She collected her things from his living room before walking her way outside and into her own unit. Ivan knocked on her door for a few minutes until she said from the other side.

"Please. Stop it. I need some time alone."

The knocks stopped, and a few seconds later, another door was shut.

—-

Just months ago, it was Christian who was the cause of Elaine's sleepless nights. It was him who was the reason why she cried and continuously asked herself of what's wrong with her and why do people find it so hard to love her. It was him who was the reason why she didn't want to wake up to face another day and tempted her to just laze on her bed, feeling as if all the energy had been sucked out from her.

But now, just a few months later, Ivan had been occupying her mind much more than she expected he would.

He is a good man. He's nice, funny, responsible, smart, and even good-looking—a complete catch if she dared say. When she first saw him, all sweaty and panting from carrying heavy boxes, she just saw him as just another attractive man who happened to be her neighbor and nothing else. Admittedly, she even forgot about him until their embarrassing encounter at the church. That was how it was, but because of one date, it turned into something more.

Elaine found herself genuinely enjoying Ivan's company as they spent more time together. It started from scheduled dates and movie nights until they found themselves into a routine of being together every other day, whether it was to just talk, share about their day, or watch movies.

It was a routine that they easily adapted too—they never forced themselves into it nor did they set fixed days and to-do lists whenever they meet. Day by day, Elaine found herself thinking of her ex-boyfriend less, and whenever she did, it was to smile at the memories they shared and never to wallow in the sadness and the gaping hole he made when he left.

As Ivan made her feel light-hearted, carefree and secured, she found herself forgetting about the heartbreaking nights, about the times when she went back to an empty home, and about the thrown away pictures and gifts. With Ivan, she felt that she could try again, that she could, maybe, fall in love again.

But it seemed that Ivan thought otherwise. She could still see how hurt he was when he talked about his ex-wife inviting him to her wedding. She could remember how tightly clenched his fists were and how much he was trembling in anger. It was a sight she never expected to see from the usually composed man.

When she asked that question she wasn't hoping for an absolute no. They were married and she knew that he must have felt so strongly for her to ask for her hand. But at the least, she was expecting something along the lines of 'I'm doing fine' or 'I'm getting over it' and it would have sufficed, for her at least.

If anything, it made her realize how much she was wearing her heart on her sleeve yet again. She wasn't in love with him, not yet at least, but she knew she was on her way. All along, she thought he felt the same, that he was moving forward and trying to forget his past heartbreak, just like her. Elaine thought that a part of him had thought about her in a romantic way, that she might be someone who he can ideally like, but then again, those were just Elaine's assumptions.

The problem with her, as always, were her hopes and baseless assumptions. These always manage to fuck her emotionally—big time. She just never learned.

—

Ivan tried to contact her in the following days but she was resolved on avoiding him for a few days. She was aware that she was being immature but she deemed herself unprepared.

Every day, she recited every line she could say once they managed to talk. She imagined different scenarios and how she would react to them and what she should say. She admitted, most of her though-of situations were bad. She wasn't too hopeful that they would be returning back to the friendly yet flirty camaraderie they had formed.

Elaine was far from being level-headed. When it came to feelings, she was like an open book. She never tried to hide what she was feeling nor did she ever lie about it. So when one day, while standing on the train, hand clasped tightly on the handrail, and a man stood behind her and asked "Will you be my girlfriend?" she broke down in tears and attracted the attention of other commuters.

Among all the scenarios she imagined in her head, this wasn't how it was supposed to be. He wasn't supposed to show out of nowhere and tell her things she has been wishing to hear for weeks in the middle of a crowded train. She tried to stop her tears but the various emotions overwhelmed her.

Ivan had panicked, wiping away her tears furiously with his fingers and then the sleeves of his sweater. He was expecting her to shriek or push him away or to give him the finger, but this wasn't in his imagined reactions.

When the train stopped at the next station, he gently guided Elaine out and continued hushing her. Her cries were now reduced to sobs and Ivan cursed at himself for making her cry.

Once she was calm, she smacked him hardly on his chest, before saying a garbled "Yes."

For a while, Ivan was confused why she said that but broke into a large grin when he realized the implication.

Overjoyed, he grabbed her face with both hands and kissed her, right in the middle of the station, with some bystanders looking away from the scene. The kiss was chaste yet sweet. Their lips glided smoothly against each other and for a while, Ivan was tempted to press harder, which was futile when Elaine pushed him.

"But," Elaine sniffed and shushed him with a finger on his lips. "Explain."

"Could I take you home first? It's starting to get cold," he gestured at her working clothes—a thin blouse and a pencil skirt—and led them outside and hailed a cab.

There was a deafening silence throughout the ride home and their way up in the elevator, but Ivan never let go of her hand the whole time.

He led them to his unit instead of Elaine's and she was about to protest but he insisted.

He pushed her until she was seated on the sofa and he sat beside her as closely as possible. She squirmed in her seat and he gave her some space, rubbing his neck sheepishly.

He reached for her hand and turned his body towards her.

He started with a deep breath before launching to his long narrative. "That night, when you asked me if I still loved her, I was sure that my answer was no," He brought a hand up when he saw that she was about to interrupt him.

He continued once she silently agrees to keep on listening.

"But at the same time, I can't say it. It sounds more real once you say it out loud doesn't it? Am I making any sense?" He chuckled. Meanwhile, Elaine responded that yes, she understands because she felt the same thing with Christian.

"We were a couple since high school, and then through college. Most people called us the ideal couple and were just waiting for us to get married. It was as if there was no other way out of it but to build our own family. So I did ask for her hand in marriage and she said yes." Ivan heaved a deep breath, composing his next words in his mind.

"But as soon as we started living together, something felt...weird. A year later, I realized how used we are to being together. We were so used to seeing each other, to doing things together that it only seemed natural that we got married. I realized that maybe, we took marriage for granted, and it was a hurried decision merely out of obligation because of the people's expectations."

"We started to drift away from each other then. In the back of my mind, I knew she was thinking the same thing. When I saw her with another man, it hurt me—not because I still love her but because I was at least expecting that we wouldn't reach that point where we would hide secrets behind each other's backs—especially a lover at that."

"I saw red and then I found myself furious. I was angry at her but more at myself for letting us be trapped in that situation. When we decided on the divorce, it was heartbreaking but it felt like a burden

I never knew I had was lifted from me. It felt liberating." He paused, tightening his hold on Elaine's hand. Elaine returned the gesture, egging him to go on.

"I admit. It still hurts. But not because I still love her but more from the fact that I spent so many years thinking I was happy but realized that I wasn't. It was hard coming to terms with that: that I forced myself to think that everything was alright when it wasn't. And then suddenly, she told me the news that she's getting married and practically screaming at me that she's found her happiness. I'm happy for her. We've been together for so long that I can't even bear thinking of hating her. But then I thought of myself and my sorry state of a coward who can't even ask you to be mine and I was enraged because I felt that it was unfair. I thought that I deserve my own happiness too." His voice trembled then and he blinked repeatedly as his eyes began to get misty.

Elaine knelt beside him and pulled his head to her chest, rubbing his back consolingly at the confession.

"I'm sorry if I hurt you. Because all these just came crashing on me and I suddenly couldn't answer. I didn't know where to start. It felt too much." She felt a wetness on her arm and hugged him more tightly. If she could only take a part of the pain he was feeling, she would do it.

"I'm sorry for assuming the worst, and for not giving you a chance to explain." She muttered, kissing a spot in his head to reassure him that she was there, and she won't be leaving anytime soon.

Ivan retreated and pulled her into his lap, resting his forehead against hers. "I'm sorry for giving you the chance to assume the worst, then. If anything, I just really want to say how much I like you and how much you make me happy." He gave her a peck and kept his lips there, feeling the smile forming on his lips.

"I'm really glad I met you. I'd do anything I could so you could forget him completely."

Elaine shook her head no in protest. "No, Ivan. We will work together so we could heal completely. This is no you helping me, nor me helping you. This is us helping each other," she said, gazing into his eyes lovingly.

He smiled a smile that reached his eyes, the one that Elaine absolutely adored, before replying. "I love the sound of that."

END

REACH FOR HIM

SARAH LOVE

Bridget Perry flipped down the visor against the afternoon sun as she steered in sweeping curves along the coastal road. She drew in her breath sharply. Her wrists hurt. She glanced at her wrists which were bruised and swollen and then averted her eyes. She didn't want to be reminded of them or of the event that caused them.

For the umpteenth time that day, tears welled in her eyes and spilled down her cheeks. Not even the stunning beauty of an Australian sunset could distract her from the heaviness in her heart. Images of her ex, came unbidden to her mind; his fathomless black eyes and raven hair falling long and wavy down his muscled back; his teeth white against swarthy skin. Bridget's breath caught in her throat. "Jackson," she whispered through her tears. She sighed one long shuddering miserable breath. Why was she crying over that two-timing, heartless pig anyway? Because I don't know how to be by myself, was the honest answer.

Bridget squinted and slowed down. With the sun at this angle she could barely see a few feet in front of her. She rounded the bend at a crawl and noticed a small motel sitting back away from the road, shrouded in thick foliage; a wooden sign peeped out from behind a heavy overhang of magenta flowers; Bougainvillea lodge it said in a cursive blue letters. Suddenly, Bridget wanted nothing more than to stop at here away from the sun, where she would be able to rest and recuperate. She pulled in and the gravel crunched in welcome as she parked the car. She stifled a groan. Sitting in the car for fourteen hours straight had done its work on her muscles. As she pulled herself out of the car and stretched her arms behind her head, she caught a glimpse of the view. Bougainvillea lodge had a perfect position facing the beach, which was, to her great relief, devoid of crowds, except for a lone walker and his dog and a young couple with small children paddling in the shallows.

The woman behind the counter welcomed her with just the right balance of warmth and respect for privacy that she needed, giving her a key and reminding her that dinner would be served at the restaurant at six. With slow deliberate steps, Bridget carried her bag, packed in such haste the night before and now she realized depressingly light, to her room. Not doubting that she had left most of her best clothes and belongings behind, she looked around the room. Nothing special, she thought, but adequate for her needs. The bathroom looked clean enough and turning back the bed, she was pleased to find crisp white cotton sheets. Right now that was all the mattered, a hot shower and sleep.

With her clothes strewn across the bathroom floor, she winced with pleasure as the hot water pummelled her tired and sore shoulders. She lathered up every part of her body and scrubbed. What she was scrubbing away she wasn't sure, but the need to be clean was overwhelming. There was more crying, but this time, the tears were more from relief than sadness. It felt good to be alone where no one could reach her or find her. She was so tired. It was all she could do to dry herself off and pull on some clean underwear and a t-shirt and crawl, exhausted into bed.

When she opened her eyes the room was dark with one brilliant shard of light spilling through a gap in the heavy drapes. Bridget reached out and felt her way over the bedside table for her phone. Her home screen glowed with a photo of Jackson during their holiday to Bali the year before. She frowned at it and focused on the time instead – 11.am! She flopped back on the pillows for a minute, amazed at how long she had slept. She lay there listening to her body. She felt relaxed and for the first time in ten months, safe.

Last April, Jackson had walked into her life and turned it upside down. He was mesmerizing in his masculine beauty. She was the envy of women wherever they went; she saw it in their eyes. Women, who ordinarily were shy and mousey, became predatory and catlike in his presence. He was talented, funny, and charming in public; but it hadn't taken long for her to realize that behind closed doors he was a cold, narcissistic bully. Ten months of verbal put-downs had left her believing that no other man would ever tolerate her the way he did. She had suspected cheating but had never been able to find any definitive evidence. He didn't need to cheat behind her back anyway. He was happy enough to flirt with other women right under her nose. On the rare occasion she called him out on it, he would jeer and tell her she was lucky to be with him and to leave if she didn't like it.

She didn't like it, but she didn't dare leave. Her best friend Nick had voiced his disapproval over and over. The image of him clenching his large, usually gentle, hands in frustration, came to mind. Dear, loyal Nick, with his lanky frame, round blue eyes, and freckled upturned nose, exactly the same as it had been when they played together as five-year-olds. He had always been there and she couldn't imagine the world without him in it. Some people winked and hinted that they would one day end up together, but she had always laughed at the idea. Nick was so safe. She knew him possibly better than she knew herself sometimes and she wanted mystery and adventure. As a result, her attention was too readily arrested by men who were exciting and unavailable in some way.

"It ticks me off," Nick had grumbled one day a few weeks into her relationship with Jackson. They were sitting on her couch watching re-runs of Seinfeld and eating chips.

"What ticks you off?"

"You, and other women too, always gushing slavishly over wankers like Jackass, I mean Jackson." He smiled wickedly. "What is it with women and bad boys? Do you actually want to be treated like crap?"

Bridget threw a cushion at Nick's head messing up the top of his straight brown hair. "He's not that bad!" She dodged the cushion on its return flight. "I don't know why but there's just something irresistible about a man who might not hang around. Knowing that he might go, but he's choosing to stay with me is sort of exciting, y'know?"

Nick's expression was incredulous. "No, I don't know! Bridge' that's the most ludicrous idea. The guy doesn't care about you! He puts you down! People don't do that to people they love, can't you see that?"

"He's had a rough life!" she countered. "His dad was a deadbeat. His mom had different men parading through his childhood. He didn't get shown much love and I want to make up for that. I think I can heal him if I love him enough."

Nick had stared at her long and hard, finally pulling her to him in a warm hug. "That isn't love Bridget. That's not how love works. Love isn't a one-way thing. It's like water." He pulled back and looked Bridget in the face. "Love is like water and people are like sponges. If you pour love into someone they should soak it up like a sponge, but if a person is like a rock, then the love just splashes and runs off the side getting wasted on the ground. Jackson's heart is a rock. You're wasting your love on him."

He had gone home after that and Bridget had thought about his analogy many times since then. It had all come to a head when last night after work, she had gone into their bathroom and found a woman's earring in the sink. She had confronted Jackson about it when he got home drunk in the early hours of the next morning, and instead of lying or being ashamed, he had mocked her and told her that the earring woman was here to stay and she could take it or leave it. She had screamed and thrown herself at him in a panicked rage and that was when he had grabbed her by the wrists twisting them cruelly and making her sink to the floor, a defeated wreck. She had packed a hurried bag and left there and then, not thinking or looking back and now 30 hours later she was here, alone, and finally free.

Pulling back the drapes of her motel room revealed a glorious Summer's day. From her window, the water glistened and the sand glowed white in the sun. It was much busier today. What had seemed like an empty country road the night before was now fringed with parked cars baking in the heat. Families strolled up and down and from the beach; the sounds of laughter and excited yelps carried across to her window.

Bridget threw on a pair of lavender shorts and a white cheesecloth peasant blouse. She looked at herself critically in the mirror. Her eyes still had a residue of puffiness from all the crying and over-sleeping but she didn't feel like wearing make-up. Her face stared back at her in solemn comradery. At 27, Bridget could still boast clear, olive skin with a smattering of freckles. Her best features apparently, were her large hazel eyes and long auburn hair. She curled her lip; obviously, Jackson didn't think they were that great. Before she could let her thoughts wander gloomily down that road, she pulled herself away from the mirror, grabbed her bag and left the room.

The air was balmy on her skin and the sound of her sandals slapping against the cool tiles brought a delicious sensation of Summer holidays bubbling up inside her. It seemed like the real Bridget was struggling up in revolt against the old, Jackson oppressed, Bridget, desperate to make a comeback. The lady behind the desk welcomed her with a smile.

"Nice day for it," she beamed. "Heading down to the beach?"

"Yep, just going for a stroll. It's busier than I expected it to be."

"That's because the agricultural show is on in Bluegum this week. When people get too hot traipsing around the showgrounds they inevitably end up here at Opal Bay to cool off. Are you going to the show today?"

Bridget let her mind wander for a moment. She imagined the showgrounds packed with hot sweaty people, crying children, loud music, and smelly livestock. She shook her head, smiling. "No, I think I'll just enjoy a peaceful day on the beach, thanks. How much are those straw hats?"

"That'll put you back ten dollars, love."

Bridget chose a broad-brimmed straw hat with a yellow and white polka-dot band. As she closed the door of the reception office behind her, she was hit with a wall of heat. In the scramble of departure, she hadn't thought to pack things like sunscreen. Without it, she was going to end the day red as a lobster, but throwing caution to the wind, she stepped out into the day with a 'come what may' attitude. She followed the sounds of laughter, seagulls, and surf across the road and through a scrubby pathway cut through the sand, slowing down against the resistance of the sand, panting a little at the effort. A couple of pre-teen boys hurtled past her, laughing like hyenas. They missed her by inches, covering her with sand in the process. She laughed out loud. She couldn't be angry. Their innocence was unapologetically refreshing.

An enticing aroma wafted over to her from a food stand that had been set up on the beach under a canopy. It was a sausage sizzle. Bridget's stomach growled; she hadn't given food a second thought since leaving Jackson, and now, all of a sudden, she felt that she could devour an entire side of beef. Two long lines of hungry beachgoers had formed at the stand, so Bridget took her place behind an elderly woman baked brown and wrinkled from a lifetime spent on Aussie beaches. Everyone was buying as much as they could in one go, and the line was moving slowly, so Bridget found herself watching the other people in the queue.

In the line next to her and a few places ahead, a tall person caught her eye. Bleached blond hair over a pair of broad tanned shoulders, tapering down to slim hips in turquoise board shorts made her smile in appreciation. She hoped he would turn around so that she could see his face. Come on, she urged mentally, turn around just a little bit. As if he heard her thoughts, the tall man turned and looked straight at her with startling blue eyes. He held her gaze just for a second and then turned back. Bridget felt like she had been hit by a sledgehammer. A very gorgeous, beach-babe kind of sledgehammer. "Just like Captain America," she murmured inwardly.

"You're too right about that, love."

Startled, Bridget looked down to see the old lady beaming up at her. "Did I say that out aloud?" she gasped, mortified.

"Yeah, but who could blame you?" The old lady looked dreamily over at the handsome man and sighed. "If I was fifty years younger, he'd be in trouble, that's all I can say."

Bridget giggled and chatted with the old lady until at last, she got to the top of the line and bought her food which she ate at the base of some dunes further up the beach. Every now and then she would search the water to locate the tall blond. He was easy to spot in his turquoise board shorts out in the surf catching a few waves. It was nice to watch him unobserved from her vantage point. Occasionally, she would acknowledge a twinge of guilt over looking at a man other than Jackson, and then the truth would come slamming down like a judge's gavel. Verdict - Jackson isn't yours, Bridget. He never was. He doesn't love you. It's over. Then the real Bridget would push again from within. The indignant Bridget, the proud Bridget, encouraging and boosting her confidence a smidgen further. It was a sensation she welcomed back with open arms.

From her spot on the beach, the sapphire-blue water looked so tempting, she regretted not bringing something to swim in. But there was no reason not to get at least a little bit wet. She unfolded her stiff muscles and made her way down to the water's edge, wading in till the water came up to her knees. Keeping to the shallows, Bridget splashed along, stopping here and there to pick up a pretty shell which she tucked into the pocket of her shorts. An urgent shout somewhere behind her, made Bridget turn around. Further back where she had been sitting, a woman was screaming for help. Some people were stopping and looking at her with concern. Although Bridget couldn't hear, she could see they were asking her what was the matter. Others, Bridget noticed in angry amazement, had pulled their phones out and were recording the scene. And then Bridget saw it, at the woman's feet, a small limp body lay in the sand. Without a second thought, Bridget started to run. Where were the lifeguards? She'd seen their watch tower about five hundred meters up the beach. As she ran, she shouted at anyone who would listen. "Call the lifeguards! Unconscious child on the beach!" Bridget fell momentarily and was up in an instant, sprinting as hard as her legs would carry her. Out of the corner of her eye, another figure was running up from the water. It was Turquoise board shorts, hurtling along like some kind of superhero toward the screaming woman. Bridget arrived panting heavily at the woman's side. What she saw made her heart sink.

"My boy! Help my boy! A Bluebottle stung him. I think he's allergic!"

Without answering, Bridget sank to her knees by the little boy. He looked about five and his lips were blue. Across his torso and upper arms were the tell-tale red welts of a jellyfish sting. Bluebottles were painful but not usually dangerous. If this child was experiencing anaphylactic shock, he could die. She shouted again for someone to get the lifeguards and then, summoning everything she had learned in First Aid at school, she immediately began CPR. Beside her, the boy's mother was kneeling over them now with silent tears coursing down her face. Bridget was also aware of Turquoise board shorts beside her assessing the situation.

"What's going on? Are you trained?" he was asking Bridget. She shook her head.

"Bluebottle sting. Possible allergic reaction."

"Then let me help; you breathe; I'll do the compressions."

Together, the two of them continued to work on the little boy with the hushed, expectant crowd watching on. Bridget wondered if they were making any difference at all when finally, after what seemed an age, the crowd parted for two lifeguards, who quickly assessed the situation, and took over. Relieved, Bridget and Turquoise board shorts, moved away, shaking and exhausted from the adrenaline coursing through their veins. They stood leaning on each other watching on as the lifeguards worked. Bridget found herself praying repeatedly; please God, don't let him die? The silence around them was heavy, broken only by the sounds of the lifeguards working on the little boy and the mournful call of gulls. The waves rolled into shore rhythmically as though they were trying to drum life back into the child.

A sudden noise split the quiet. A wet splutter and a weak cough, and then thank heaven, a louder choke and cough, and then a cry! An unearthly wail burst from the little boy's mother as she realized her son wasn't dead and a cheer rose from the crowd. Bridget found herself turning to congratulate Turquoise board shorts only to find that he had left. When did that happen? She scanned the beach without success. He was nowhere to be seen. Bridget turned back to watch the little boy being carried off on a stretcher. His mother paused a moment to hug her and thank her.

"Thank you so much, I think you saved my little boy's life! Please thank your boyfriend for me okay?" She hurried off to follow her son and the crowd dispersed. Bridget stood there, suddenly deflated after the intensity of the experience. For some reason, the beach had lost its attraction and her thoughts turned to the Agricultural show. Maybe it wouldn't be such a bad idea to go for an hour or two?

Half an hour later she was entering the town of Bluegum having first gone back to the motel for a change of clothes. It was easy to find the showgrounds. Street signs directing the traffic to the show were on every corner. Pedestrians seemed to have only one destination, and when she pulled into carpark she could see that there was still a bit of a queue to buy tickets. Bridget entered the grounds through an old-fashioned turnstile joining the throng of hot and tired patrons trying to navigate the crowds. The festival was in full swing with Ferris wheels and Dodgem cars, side shows, and fairy floss stands. She passed huge barns and stables which housed all of the prize winning livestock. The smell of manure wafted out making Bridget's nostrils twitch. Ugh, she thought, immediately regretting her decision. What she needed was somewhere she could just sit and be entertained for a while. Reflecting on childhood visits to the Royal Melbourne Show, a particularly fond memory popped into her head. The Grand Arena, of course! She would go and watch the parades of animals, the horse tricks, the clowns and daredevil acts and maybe even wait till evening for the firework display.

Bridget decided to just follow the general flow of pedestrians, stopping here and there to look at displays on the way. On the corner of an intersection was an old fashioned American style diner where they sold snacks and takeaway food. As she passed she could see into the diner. People were sitting, chatting and eating in the leather upholstered booths. She was hungry, but she wasn't in the mood for hotdogs. She was just about to cross the road and stop at a place selling kebabs when out of the corner of her eye she glimpsed a flash of blond hair. Bridget stopped dead in her tracks causing a man and woman to crash into her from behind.

"Watch where you're bloody going!"

Bridget wasn't sure if she apologized or not. She actually didn't care, because there, shoving a hot dog into his beautiful mouth, was Turquoise board shorts, in the American Diner! Before embarrassment, fear, or good judgment could stop her, she had climbed the few steps and walked through the glass doors. He didn't look up; he was too engrossed in his meal to notice. Bridget found herself standing by his booth with a shy grin on her face.

"Hi."

Turquoise board shorts started. His wide blue eyes opening even wider at the sight of her. "Hey!" He struggled to stand up but got hooked up on the corner of the table, jabbing his hip and making him wince. He smiled through the pain, extending his hand to her. "Hey, it's you, the CPR girl!"

"Yep, it's me. I was just passing and happened to see you. You left so quickly at the beach, I was hoping to introduce myself and thank you for your help... do you mind if I join you?"

"No, not at all, no worries, I'd enjoy you... I mean, that would be nice."

Bridget slid into the booth across from him and they appraised each other for a couple of seconds.

"I'm Bridget, and you are?"

"Daniel, Daniel Inglis."

"You say that like you're James Bond or something." Bridget ran her hand through her hair and twiddled with a loose curl at the end. "Actually, you did look a bit like James Bond running up the beach like that to save the day."

Daniel grimaced. "Oh, no, did I? How embarrassing. Well, you were doing a bit of a Wonder woman yourself. It was quite impressive."

Bridget laughed. "We should have our own show!" They were interrupted by a waitress who took Bridget's order. Bridget continued, "So, do you live locally?"

"No." Just on a trip for work and passing through. You?"

Bridget sighed, wondering how much she should say. "No, I'm not local. I guess you could say I'm a city girl looking to make a sea change. I'm on the hunt for a new place to establish some roots and start a new life." She stopped wondering if she had said too much. Daniel seemed to understand and didn't pry any further.

"That sounds quite an appealing idea actually. I think we all could benefit from starting afresh once in a while. What do you do for a crust?"

"I'm a teacher, and I run an online business writing résumés and cover letters." She narrowed her eyes at him, thinking. "Hmm, let me see if I can guess what you are. You look like you could be a doctor... am I close?"

"Well, I am in the business of taking care of people so you're right there. I guess you could say I'm a social worker of sorts."

Bridget absorbed the information in happy disbelief; this guy was almost too good to be true. A social worker meant he was someone who cared about people, not only that, he was polite, unpretentious, and of course drop dead gorgeous. And the best thing about him, she decided, was that he was the absolute opposite of Jackson. All of the feelings of longing and hurt about Jackson dissolved right there in that diner booth. It fizzled into nothing so quickly she was shocked into stark realization of what she had been succumbing herself to for the past ten months. The understanding that not only had Jackson never loved her but that she had never loved him was as plain as the nose on her face. Across from her Daniel was looking at her with one eyebrow raised and a crooked smile.

"By the look on your face, my job description doesn't meet with your approval."

"What? Oh, no! I think it's a wonderful, honorable kind of work... No, if I looked odd, I was thinking of how different you are to someone I know."

Daniel was quiet, focusing his attention on removing the cherry from the top of his Ice-cream Sundae. It slipped off the edge of his spoon and slid down the side of his glass onto the plate; his eyes traveled from his plate to the bruises on her wrists. "Is that someone you're running away from?" His blue eyes looked up and held her in a questioning gaze for a moment before licking the ice-cream off his spoon. Bridget pulled her hands back under the table, her voice was mildly indignant.

"You could say that. But not running. Yesterday I was dragging myself away, but today I can say it's over. I've left and I'm never going back."

"Good."

Bridget looked up at him. He was looking at her steadily, knowingly. She took a deep breath. "And now I'm all alone like Nellie No Friends at the Bluegum Agricultural Show. I don't suppose I could twist your arm to spend the day with me? I'd feel silly going on the roller coaster by myself."

Daniel hesitated, but only for an instant. "Consider it twisted," he said with a grin.

They spent the rest of the afternoon having more fun than Bridget had experienced in what seemed like years. Daniel was funny and intelligent and insightful with an air of confidence that was deeply appealing. Never once did he utter a sexist remark or blurt obscenities or look her over like a piece of steak, like Jackson would have. In contrast, he was the consummate gentleman, helping her onto rides, walking ahead of her in the crowds to shield her from being jostled, and opening doors for her. Once or twice when standing in a queue she would feel his hand brush against hers or his hand on her arm protectively.

After the sun went down, they took their dinner to the Grand Arena to watch the fireworks. As they stood staring mesmerized like little children at the display, Bridget felt Daniel's arms slip around her waist from behind. She leaned into him, enjoying the hard warmth of his chest against her back and his mouth near her ear. Like this, it was difficult to concentrate on the fireworks because there were fireworks of another sort going off inside her. But, fighting to the surface of her consciousness, a small voice came unsolicited from the deepest recesses of her mind. It was a voice of – what was it a voice of, caution perhaps, or was it good judgment? Don't rush it was telling her, but the voice quickly became garbled and indistinct as she pushed it back where it came from.

Their conversation became slower and quieter after that. A different kind of language had taken over. Words were replaced by holding hands and shy caresses. As they walked back to Daniel's car the air was electric with the question – what next? There was a choice to be made. Was Daniel making the same choice? What was he thinking? She looked at him sideways out of the corner of her eye, as he fumbled with the car keys. He's nervous too, she realized. The trip home in the car was silent except for snippets of polite small talk. Neither of them wanted to destroy the mood, they were heading toward one conclusion for the night and they both knew it.

Daniel walked Bridget to her door; the light above had blown and they were standing, conveniently, in the shadows, away from prying eyes. She wondered if there was any point going through the usual end of date etiquette of thanking Daniel for a nice time, the invitation for a nightcap etc. He was still behind her, so she turned to face him and lifted her face to his. What she saw on his face startled her somewhat. His eyes that had been bright and blue all day, were now almost black; his pupils dilated to their fullest. There was an intensity there that both frightened her and bound her, unable to look away. She ran her tongue over her lips in anticipation and his eyes dropped to her mouth. When he spoke, his voice was hoarse.

"You have the most beautiful mouth."

Bridget's lips curled into a softly parted smile and she leaned in closer. He was going to kiss her. She closed her eyes and waited, focusing all of her attention on her mouth in anticipation. The night breeze on her moist lips was cool, and then his lips were there, warm, firm and full on hers. His arms went around her and lifted her up so that her toes were barely touching the ground. He held her so effortlessly that she let herself relax into the kiss. This was more like it; so much nicer than Jackson's hurried, rough embraces. A new idea came to her mind, wouldn't it be nice to leave it here and to let it remain sweet and romantic, to softly say goodnight and close the door in anticipation of another date? But as Daniel's kisses became more urgent, her resolve began to weaken. Self-control had never been her forte. She broke the kiss and pulled away. "Stay with me?" she whispered. Daniel nodded and followed her into the dark motel room and closed the door behind him with a click.

She was in a strange house with a corridor flanked by walls with garish lime wallpaper. The color made her nauseous. Along the walls were dozens of doors leading to dark rooms, which she entered panicked and fevered, looking for something, but she didn't know what. "I'm running out of time, running out of time!" The words ran in a loop over and over in her head, but the further she ran down the corridor the smaller it got and every room became more cramped, stifling her and filling her with desperate dread, until finally she was wedged tight and suffocating at the pointed end of the corridor, curled up in a ball.

Bridget woke with a start sitting bolt upright in the dawn light, covered in perspiration and her chest heaving. The dream, which was a reoccurring one, was still fresh in her mind, but she knew if she waited a minute it would fade. Then she remembered Daniel. Jerking her head around, she stared at the other side of the bed. It was rumpled, but empty. She scanned the room. He was gone. He had left nothing behind. A small white object on the sheet beside her caught her eye. It was the butt of a ticket for the roller coaster ride from the day before. Bridget lay back on the pillow staring with unseeing eyes at the tiny shred of paper. Last night had not been what she had expected. She had expected to wake up full and replete with Prince Charming breathing softly beside her. Instead, the experience had been furtive and intense. Daniel's set jaw and black eyes swam before her. There had been nothing magical about last night as she had hoped. A ball of regret began to form in the pit of her stomach. It was too soon after Jackson. She had known that last night. Why couldn't she just say no to men? Nick was going to have something to say about this when she told him.

The thought of unburdening herself to Nick gave her some comfort. The red digits on the bedside clock glowed 6:23; a bit early but he'd be getting up to get ready for work soon anyway. His phone rang out. She was hesitating, wondering whether she should try again when her phone began to vibrate; Nick's photo coming up on her screen. She swiped the screen with relief.

"Hi, it's me." Nick's voice was heavy with sleep.

"Hi, me, sorry for waking you up. I just needed to talk to my best mate."

"Hmm. Are you okay?"

Bridget could hear him yawning and stretching on the other end of the line.

"Yeah, I'm safe but just depressed and sick of myself. I'm so stupid, Nick."

"What happened?"

"I met this guy."

Nick moaned in exasperation. "What? A guy? Bridget, it has been three days since you left Jackson. Three days! You have no business getting involved with any guy for any reason right now. And then, realizing that he hadn't heard her out, his tone softened. "I'm sorry, I didn't give you a chance to explain, go ahead."

"No, you are right to be exasperated. I met a guy, a really nice guy, but I rushed things and he ended up staying the night. He didn't hurt me, it's not like he's a serial killer or anything, I just feel stupid for being so desperate and having no self-control." Her voice began to quiver with emotion. "I've forgotten what's good about me, Nick. I'm just sick of myself."

Nick didn't answer right away and when he did his voice was tender. "There's plenty that's good about you Bridget." But you have to learn how to be alone and happy before you can be with someone and be happy. There are good men out there, but you have to be willing to change your expectations. My mom always said that the best apples were at the top of the tree and the hardest ones to find and she was right." The silence on Bridget's end told Daniel she was crying. "You're the best friend I've ever had Bridget and I hate to see you sad. I think you're crazy sometimes, but I'll always be here for you. What are you going to do now? Will you come home?"

A part of Bridget wanted to go home, but she had left for a reason, to learn about herself and to reinvent herself where nobody had any preconceived notions about her. "No Nick. I'm going to find somewhere to settle up here and make a go of it. Thanks for listening to me, you're my bestie and I love you." Nick's voice was soft in reply. "I love you too."

Once Bridget was dressed, she went into Bluegum and bought some supplies, including a map of Queensland. Her motel room had been cleaned and the bed made when she returned. It matched her mood. She felt energized. It was finally time to leave her old life and her old mistakes behind her. But she needed a place to lay down roots. She spread the map out over the small circular dining table, holding it in place with the pepper and salt shakers on two corners and the sugar bowl on another. She rummaged in her shopping bag and ripped open a crackling plastic package containing a brand new red felt pen. She leaned close to locate Bluegum on the map and placed a small red dot there, then, raising the pen like a dagger, she shut her eyes and dropped her arm, randomly onto the map. It had landed about two inches away from the Bluegum dot. "Good, not too far to drive then," she muttered. She squinted and shifted her head to the side to see the name of her new hometown. Currawong about an hour away from Bluegum. She liked the name of the town immediately. Currawong, one of her favourite Australian birds, like a large black crow with patches of white on the tips of its wings was a good omen to her. She had no idea what was at Currawong, maybe she would arrive to find nothing, but she was going to go anyway and see what happened.

The trip was uneventful, but as she drew closer to her destination, she was pleased to see green fields, rather than the harsh yellow bushlands she had been expecting. A large sign on the side of the road said: "You are entering Currawong – pop 5000." She instantly felt like she had gone back 60 years. The houses were vintage weatherboard houses, circa 1950 with immaculate gardens and pristine driveways. Many of the homes were on acreage with a couple of horses grazing back from the road. The main strip was fairly modern but it only took a few minutes to drive through the center of town and then she was back out in the country.

Being careful to keep to the speed limit, she headed for the motel she had booked into back in Opal Bay. "Turn left in 100 meters," said the ever polite voice on her GPS. As Bridget turned left she admired a sweet old bluestone church on the corner. A group of parishioners were in the front weeding and tending the garden. They were an assorted group of moms, dads, children, teenagers and old age pensioners, all working together in a steady rhythm. With her windows rolled down, she could hear laughter and chatter coming from the group. Something inside her wished she could park the car and join in; there seemed to be such a spirit of belonging amongst them.

That night as she lay in her motel bed, looking through the newspaper for rental properties, she reflected on the little church again. As a little girl, her parents had taken her every week to church and she had enjoyed their time together as a family. She remembered the solemn feelings she held in her heart, even as a child, for the church and everything it stood for. She missed the reverent prayers, the quiet atmosphere, and the hope it all inspired. Maybe that was what was missing in her life? How far had she drifted away from her core beliefs? How much had she let the whims and wishes of others influence her away from what she held to be true? She made the decision there and then, that she would attend church services the next Sunday. Bridget felt much lighter over the next couple of days. She felt good about looking inside herself and facing her demons head on. It was nice to let the misery go and to commit to change. It felt like her soul was being washed clean in her resolve to be happy.

On Sunday morning, she dressed for church. Her packing had been abysmal with absolutely nothing that could pass as suitable for church, so the day before, she had bought herself a new dress befitting her mood. It was a crisp cotton dress with a fitted bodice and wide knee-length skirt in pale yellow. She matched it with a pair of summery slingback white stilettos and finished the look by pulling her auburn hair up into a long ponytail, making her look every bit as wholesome as she hoped she would. Looking herself over in the mirror she raised an eyebrow at her reflection. "This is it, Bridget. Don't let me down."

The walk to church seemed to be straight out of a Disney movie. The sun was shining, the birds singing, the breeze cool and refreshing. Families were walking to church together in their Sunday best. Bridget held back a little. She wanted to be the last to walk into the chapel so that she wouldn't be an object of curiosity to the others. At first, when she entered the chapel she was blinded in the cool dark after the brilliance of the outside sunshine. The chapel was nearly full friends and families in soft conversation, waiting for the reverend to emerge from the vestry. Bridget quietly took a seat in the last pew. Thankfully nobody had noticed her yet. She sat in quiet meditation, while the organist treated them to soft prelude music. It was rare that Bridget felt confident about one of her decisions, but today, she was convinced she was in the right place.

The prelude music faded and the congregation turned their faces in unison toward the vestry door. A soft click of a door latch at the side of the chapel released a beam of yellow light from within and emerging from the light, a tall figure, so tall and broad he had to bend his head to avoid hitting the top of the door. It was a blond head. From where she sat, Bridget couldn't see his face, only the back of his blond head and his black robes. Bridget's heart began to beat quicker. There was an uncomfortable sensation bubbling up from her stomach to her throat. The reverend was looking far too familiar for her liking. Then as the organist began to play the opening hymn, he turned around to face the congregation. Bridget took an audible gasp of air. Daniel! It was Daniel!

The congregation rose from their seats in a synchronized swoosh. Somewhere on the right side of the chapel, someone dropped their hymnbook with a loud clatter, but Bridget barely heard it; the chorus of voices around her was a muffled behind the blood whooshing through her ears. She felt faint and leaned forward to rest her head on the back of the pew in front of her. Daniel, a priest? Shame and anger threatened to drown her as she remembered with embarrassment their night together. If she'd known, she would have never.... How dare he not tell her? The shame began to dissipate. He was the one breaking his vows. She wasn't party to that. She looked up at him standing at the pulpit. Was he going to stand up there and preach from the Bible now?

The hymn ended and the congregation sat, waving fans in the heat, all eyes watching Daniel in rapt expectation. Bridget was glad that the chapel was full. It was unlikely that Daniel would see her sitting down in the back row, but leaving was out of the question; firstly, he would see her leave and think her a coward and secondly, she wanted to confront him. He started to speak and Bridget, in spite of herself was impressed. He wasn't preachy at all. He spoke of kindness and acceptance, service and dedication. He told amusing anecdotes that made the congregation chuckle, he mentioned people by name, he spoke of his own weaknesses. Bridget was starting to soften. Maybe the night with her was a one-off? Maybe, like everyone else, he had weaknesses that he was trying to work through? As the hour passed, so did her indignation. She gazed at Daniel. He was beautiful she had to admit. Maybe there could be a future with him? If she were to approach him and if he were willing, they could start afresh, and she would never ask him to overstep the boundaries of his faith. Nick's words nagged at her conscience, "you have to learn to be alone." "Oh, shut up, Nick," she mumbled out loud, making the people in front of her turn and stare.

After the service, Bridget, made her way against the stream of people leaving the chapel, up towards the pulpit, where Daniel was tidying up and preparing to leave. She arrived at the front just as he was heading towards the vestry.

"Reverend Inglis?"

Daniel turned swiftly with a ready smile, which fell comically as soon as he recognized her. "Yes? Oh!"

"Surprised to see me?"

Daniel's face froze into a stiff smile, but his eyes were boring into hers heavy with meaning. He spoke in urgent tones through his stiff smile like a ventriloquist. "Can't talk now." He glanced over Bridget's shoulder at someone approaching from behind. And then she heard the sound that made her blood run cold; a little girl's voice over the din of the departing congregation.

"Daddy!"

Like an ax dropping onto the executioner's block, Bridget's expression dropped into one of quiet fury. Not this. There would be no forgiving for this! She looked over her shoulder to see a little girl of about four, with honey colored curls running toward Daniel. He stood stiffly as his daughter hugged his legs. Following the little girl was a dark haired woman with a babe in arms. The woman approached her with a friendly smile. "Hello, you must be new? I'm Carrie Inglis, welcome!" She offered her hand to Bridget who did her best to hitch a believable looking smile onto her face. Whatever had happened was not this woman's fault, and she was not going to do anything that could possibly hurt her any further. "Hi, Carrie, nice to meet you."

Carrie's face was open, gazing directly into Bridget's eyes. "It's always good to have new people join us," she turned to Daniel, "isn't it honey?" But Daniel was already half way out of the chapel with his little girl in tow. Carrie laughed. "What's his rush? He's usually hanging around talking for ages after church. So, tell me about yourself, where are you staying?" She was so genuine that Bridget found herself wavering between shock and anger at Daniel and an irresistible connection with his wife. Overriding these two emotions was an overwhelming desire to get away, to be alone where she could lick her wounds and somehow come to terms with what had happened. She jotted down her address and phone number for Carrie and then making her excuses she made her way back to the motel room. It wasn't until she was alone that the full impact of what Daniel had subjected her to hit her. All of the excuses she had tried to make for him, fell flat and lifeless. He was a liar and a cheater and cheating on one of the loveliest ladies she had ever met and only a few weeks after she'd given birth to a new baby!

Like the voice of her conscience sitting on her shoulder, Nick's voice came to her mind. "It takes two to tango," he was saying, "Daniel didn't do this on his own."

"But I didn't know he was married!" she cried out to the room at large. "Did you know anything about him before you invited him home?" came Nick's steady voice again.

Bridget looked at her phone. If she had Nick's voice berating her in her head, she may as well call him and get the confession over and done with. He was going to find out about this at some point anyway, and she really needed his advice. When he answered his voice was cautious but hopeful.

"Hey Bridget, is this call to just say hi to your best friend because you miss me, or have you got bad news?"

Bridget sighed. "Bad news. He is a priest. A married priest with two children."

"Who, what? No, not the guy from the other night? How do you know?"

"I randomly attended his church today. How's that for serendipity?"

There was silence on the line for a moment. "Maybe serendipity, or maybe a life lesson? Maybe a chance to make things right? Wow, Bridge' what a shock. What's his wife like? Did she find out?"

"She's an absolute darling. Anybody who could willingly hurt a person like her has got to have something wrong with them, and no, thankfully, she doesn't know anything."

"What are you going to do?"

Bridget asked herself the same question. What was she going to do? She felt she had been directed to this little town, and directed to the church. Should she let Daniel's presence influence her own journey? No, why should he have a say? Maybe Currawong had happier surprises up its sleeve for her. The decision formed and settled in her heart. "I'm going to stay," she answered.

The week that followed was a blur. Carrie contacted her on the Tuesday with a fabulous rental opportunity. An elderly aunt and uncle were going overseas for six months and needed a house-sitter. The situation was perfect, she wouldn't have to buy furniture, the rent was cheap and the house boasted a backyard shady with glorious, mauve, Jacarandas and a wrap-around veranda, perfect for entertaining or working on her laptop. By Thursday she had moved in and made friends with neighbors and been invited for tea. By 10 o'clock that evening she was brushing her teeth getting ready for bed and feeling appreciative and hopeful for the future.

She had just pulled on an old t-shirt and a pair of Jackson's old boxers when she heard what she thought was a quiet knock on the front door. She stopped and cocked an ear to listen. Who would be knocking this late? The neighbor's dog started to bark. Bridget mentally retraced her going-to-bed ritual, had she locked all the doors? Confident that she had, she sank down onto her bed.

There it was again. Someone was definitely knocking. Padding silent as a cat in her bare feet, she approached the front door. She let out a sigh, grateful that she had taken the time to slip the safety chain into place. Another quiet knock, this time, more urgent than the last. Bridget pressed her face against the spy hole and switched on the porch light. Daniel's face, nervous and handsome was there, staring straight at the keyhole.

Jerking her face back, Bridget took a moment to decide what to do. What on earth could he want? She imagined he probably wanted to come to beg her to stay quiet about their night together. What a creep! In one swift movement, she had yanked the door open, the safety chain stopping it from opening further than four inches.

"What are you doing here?" She peered at him through the gap with narrowed eyes.

Daniel's smile was sheepish. "Bridget, I was hoping we could talk?"

"What about?"

"Us." He tried to stare seductively through the small gap in the doorway. He looked like an idiot. "I can't forget our night together, can you?" When she said nothing, he continued. "Can I come in? I'm feeling a bit exposed here under the porch light."

Bridget couldn't believe the brazen cheek of the man. "I've got nothing to hide, Daniel, and there isn't any 'us' as you put it." Her words were as sharp as razor blades. "And you've got a bloody cheek coming here and expecting me to be complicit in hurting a beautiful person like Carrie! I'm not in the business of dating married men and even if you don't appreciate your beautiful family, I do. Now rack off, before I call Carrie and tell her everything!" She slammed the door, breathing deeply with anger. Perhaps she should tell Carrie. She didn't deserve to be treated with this kind of callous, disrespect. She deserved to be rid of Daniel. Bridget imagined with satisfaction, Carrie confronting Daniel and kicking him out on the street. But there in the background of her fantasy was a small four-year-old girl crying and a baby who would only ever know weekend visits from his father.

The picture was so sad; she knew that she would never tell. She refused to add to her list of regrets, the destruction of a family.

She didn't hear from Daniel again. In spite of the drama, Bridget felt that Currawong was going to be good for her. It filled her with pride to face her fears, to confront her weaknesses and direct her attention to the needs of others for a while. Carrie was showing her that. Every day, in one way or another, Carrie was doing something to help. It didn't matter if it was a human need or a stray animal, everyone who needed it, got a dose of her kindness and attention. It inspired Bridget to do the same.

The wet season hit Queensland earlier than usual and out of the blue. One afternoon, a couple of weeks after moving in, Bridget sat in her study, staring at the torrential downpour outside. The power was out, there was no TV, and the battery on her laptop was flat and it looked like she would be forced to indulge in a lazy afternoon curled up on the couch with a book. Her phone rang. On the other end, she could hear Carrie over the din of the rain. It sounded like she was inside a tin shed. Carrie was shouting, but Bridget could only catch intermittent words. "Help – deliver shopping – old – car- time?"

Bridget yelled back. "I couldn't really hear what you said, but if you need my help, come and get me. I'll be waiting at my place!" Bridget caught a muffled "Thanks!" and hung up the phone. Fifteen minutes later, she was in the front seat of

Carrie's car in a yellow raincoat. "Okay, what am I helping you with today?"

Carrie grabbed Bridget's hand and squeezed it. "You're an angel for coming. I just need to deliver these meals to some elderly shut-ins today. Their usual delivery service is canceled due to the rain and I couldn't bear it if they went without a meal or a friendly face today. With your help, I'll be able to get it done in half the..." A loud screeching of wheels forced them to turn in terror to their right. A truck had lost control and was sliding from the opposite lane directly into their path. Before the truck slammed into them, Bridget caught a glimpse of the desperate expression on the face of the other driver. And then there was nothing.

She was in the strange house with the corridors again. This time, there was pain. Bridget resisted. She didn't want to have this dream but have it she would. Stretching away into the distance the corridor elongated. The doors came into view, beckoning her to start searching for that elusive something. She tried to grip the walls but her hands slid off, slick and wet. Against her will, she found herself at the first door. I'm running out of time... out of time... Someone was calling her from far away, "Bridget!" they called. I can't find you! She was rummaging through the room, searching. "Bridget!" The voice was louder now, from somewhere nearby, "Please wake up!" She was frantic. Help me find you!

Bridget felt herself emerge from the coma as though traveling an elevator one floor at a time. When she got to the top, her eyes opened. All around her were blurred moving shapes and muffled sounds. Only one shape directly in front of her face stayed still. She focused on it and waited for the blurriness to go away. Gradually, the shape became more distinct, the lines sharper, it was a face. It was Nick's face, wet with tears and he was smiling. Suddenly his face was next to hers and he was sobbing. She didn't know why. But now that Nick was there, everything was going to be all right.

Nick was there every day over the next two weeks in the hospital. Bridget had a concussion, a few broken ribs, a collapsed lung and her spleen had been removed. Nick told her that she had been in a coma for three days after the accident. He had taken the first flight to Queensland and had been by her side ever since. Carrie hadn't fared so well. She was still in a coma in intensive care with multiple broken bones and a head injury.

On her day of discharge, Bridget made her way to Carrie's hospital room. Daniel was by her bedside. His face was white. He looked at Bridget with eyes frantic and bloodshot. She realized in an instant that he was already receiving his punishment, nothing she could say could make him feel worse than he did right now. So, he loved his wife after all; or was this just guilt? Perhaps it was not her place to judge. She took a few ginger steps into the room and gripped the bars at the foot of Carrie's bed.

"How is she?"

Daniel leaned his elbows on the bed and rested his face in his hands. "Not good."

"I think we may have both learned the same lesson from this experience, Daniel. Since I met Carrie I've been judging you for taking your wife for granted. But I now realize that I've been taking someone for granted too, someone who has loved me my whole life and has watched and waited patiently while I've repeatedly thrown myself at people who didn't hold a candle to him. Buddha once said, 'The trouble is; you think you have time,' well now we both know that everything that is important can be taken in an instant. There is no time to waste, we only have now." Bridget turned to go and then hesitating she murmured without looking back. "Take care Daniel, I'll keep you and Carrie in my prayers."

The sunshine was bright in her hospital room when she walked stiffly through the door. Nick had his back to her; he was packing her pajamas and underwear into a duffle bag. Bridget eased her sore body into the chair by the bed and watched him. His big hands were awkward as he fumbled with her silky underwear. His brow was furrowed, his honest, open eyes, tense with the effort, his upturned boyish nose wrinkled in determination. From under her ribs, a wave of peace and security flooded her, filling her up until her heart felt like it would burst. She let out a delighted laugh. Why hadn't she been able to see it before? All the years of pain and misery looking for Mr. Right when she had the perfect man right under her nose the whole time. "I love Nick." Saying it to herself made it all the truer. She loved Nick and when the time was right she would tell him.

"There, he said with finality, zipping up the duffle bag. Where would you like to go next, my lady?"

"Home, please, Nick," she answered, rising to her feet. "Take me home."

RECKLESSLY AMISH
SAMANTHA COLLIER

Chapter One
Loss

John puffed slightly as he walked over the plain, taking off his black hat to wipe sweat from his brow. This shouldn't be happening. Still at least twenty minutes from home. His father was going to be angry.

Well, he hadn't planned for it. When the wheel had started wobbling on the buggy as he cantered along the familiar dirt road, he had slowed down. He had done everything that he could think of to get the thing home. Yes, he knew that his father had told him to adjust it days ago, but he had just plumb forgot. And then, of course, it had completely left the axle, causing the buggy to veer off into the ditch. He didn't have anything on him to fix it. So he had left it, and started walking. The horses weren't up to bare back riding.

He knew that this was a short cut; he had heard people talking about it. Veer over the plains, rather than take the road. He was still unfamiliar with the area, but he knew enough landmarks to be okay. Well, he had no other choice. He had to get home, and quickly.

It was only supposed to be a quick trip into town, to get a few things his mother needed for the Easter dinner. They had relatives arriving for the feast, all the way from Indiana, where they had recently moved from. His parents were counting on him. And then, this had to happen.

John stopped, frowning, as he surveyed the landscape. He thought he was going the right way, but it all looked the same. With a pained sigh, he started off again. Luckily, it was a perfect spring day, not a cloud in the sky. If a trifle hot.

He set off, again. It shouldn't be too much further, surely?

And that's when he saw the figure on horseback, riding over the plain like it was being pursued by half of the state. A black horse, tall and handsome. He couldn't quite make out the rider; could just see the figure crouched over the horse, spurring it on to greater speed. Really, the person was riding the horse way too fast. Yes, it was an open plain, but John knew the hard way that there were many dips and hidden holes here. He had stepped into a couple, by accident.

If the horse stepped into one, it would lose its footing entirely, and at the speed they were going, throw the rider clean off. It would also be lucky not to break its leg, and everyone knew that was the worst thing that could happen to a horse. It would be the death of the creature.

The rider approached, still at full speed. The person could see him...surely? But it didn't slow down. Instead, it approached him with such ferocity that John instinctively dived to the left.

His hat fell off, rolling down an embankment. He got up, seething with anger. The fool had almost caused another accident. He watched as the rider reined in the horse, then turned it back toward him.

"Are you alright?" The figure atop the horse gazed down at him.

John looked up, about to give the man a piece of his mind, when the words froze on his lips. It wasn't a man. No, it was a girl, and an Amish girl, at that. Still with her prayer *kapps* on her head, although it had become slightly dislodged by the wild ride. As had her hair; instead of a neat bun, it was flowing down her back.

John gaped. He had simply never seen a girl ride like that, with no awareness of her surroundings or her appearance. Who on earth was she?

"I said, are you alright?" The girl's voice sounded impatient. Well, that took the cake. She had almost ploughed into him with her horse, and there was no apology.

John brushed off his dark pants. There were scuff marks on them; his mother was not going to be happy. He was dressed in his best clothes for the feast, not his regular work ones. This day was just getting worse.

"No thanks to you," John spat, glaring up at the girl. "What do you think you were doing, riding the horse so fast towards me?"

The girl had the gall to laugh, throwing her head back so that her hair fell down her back.

"I thought you would move," she said, her eyes glittering. "Don't worry, you were never in any danger. I've been riding horses since I could walk."

"Well, then, you should know that riding one that fast on a pock holed plain is a bad idea," John answered, sourly. He waited for the apology that was his due. But she simply looked at him, smiling bemusedly.

"Who are you?" she asked, cocking her head to the side as she assessed him. "I've never seen you before."

"John Miller," he said, stiffly. "My family has only just moved here, a month ago."

"Are you living at the old Yoder farmhouse?"

"*Jah*." He scratched his head, looking up at her. "That's where I am heading, now. The wheel came off my buggy on the road, and I was told this was a shortcut."

"A shortcut to where?" She laughed, again. "You are heading in the wrong direction. You need to go that way." She pointed west. He looked, confused. He was sure he had been going the right way.

"Well, John Miller," she laughed, grabbing the reins, "good luck!" She took off at high speed, flying back over the plain in the opposite direction.

He watched her, his jaw open, riding like the wind until she was a mere speck on the horizon.

John picked up his hat, dusty on the ground. Who on earth was she? He had never known an Amish girl to be quite so.... reckless. He was used to demure and apologetic girls, who would never ride alone, and certainly not in the way that she had. Maybe the Amish girls were different in this part of the country? He hadn't really spoken to any, not yet. His family had attended a few church services, but he hadn't really socialised. He thought of Miriam, the girl he had been sweet on back in Indiana. Miriam would never have dreamt of riding like that, and would certainly have never spoken the way that the girl had.

He eventually got to the farmhouse, his mood sour. The family were all assembled at the table, waiting for him. His father stood up, frowning, watching his son walk through the door.

"Where have you been, John?" The older man's jaw tightened.

"It is a long story," John sighed. "The wheel came off the buggy, and I had to walk over the plain. Then I almost got knocked over by a horse. A girl on a black horse, riding like the wind." He shook his head, not believing his own words.

His mother had got to her feet. "You look a mess," she said. "Go and clean up." She sat back down. "Did you say a girl on a black horse? I have heard of her. The church elders of the district have talked of her, and not in a good way."

"What is her name?" John asked. He could still picture her in his mind's eye, hair flowing, eyes glittering.

"Sarah Glick?" His mother frowned, trying to remember. "*Jah*, I am sure that is her name. She is a wild one, that is for sure. You were lucky to walk away from her unscathed by the sound of it, John."

Sarah. The wild girl, who rode like a man. Well, he would make sure that he had nothing to do with her, ever again. A girl needed to be demure, and she didn't seem to know the meaning of the word.

As John walked off to the bathroom to wash, he tried to dislodge the vision of her from his mind. But she stayed with him, all through the lunch, and the tedious rest of the day, going back to fix the buggy, his father haranguing him the whole way.

***

Sarah dismounted Racer, giving the sweating black horse a kiss on his nose. "Thank you," she whispered. "That was a wonderful ride."

She waked into the house, tossing off her *kapps* as she went. Where was Mamm?

Right at that moment, her mother walked out of the kitchen, wiping flour on her apron. She stopped short when she saw her daughter, frowning.

"Sarah," she said, through gritted teeth, "where is your *kapps*? And your hair! It has come completely undone."

Sarah laughed. "It is always does," she said, nonchalantly. "The silly *kapps* can't contain it."

"Have you been riding too fast again?" Her mother had her hands on her hips as she looked at her.

Sarah's eyes flashed. "Why do you have to keep harping on about it?" she said, her voice raised. "I like to ride fast! And so does Racer."

"Sarah, it isn't seemly..."

Sarah rounded on her mother. "Why?" she shouted. "I have been hearing this forever! Who says that just because I am a girl I can't ride fast?"

Her mother sighed, closing her eyes. "We have talked about it many times," she said. "A girl in our community has to be meek, or at least not as wild as you are. You want to stay in our community, don't you?"

"*Jah*," admitted Sarah, breathing heavily. "You know that I do! I just can't understand why I can't be myself. Why are there all these silly rules and regulations? Why can a boy do what he likes but a girl can't?"

Her mother sighed, again. "It is just the way it is," she whispered. "It has always been that way. If you choose to be in our community, you must be respectful. People already gossip about you too much. It hurts your father, and myself."

Sarah rolled her eyes. "Small minded people," she spat. "Why do you care what they say?" She turned away, walking to the stairs. "I have to change."

Her mother watched her walk away, in despair. "Sarah," she called. "Rebecca needs you to mind the children, tomorrow."

Sarah's hand tightened on the balustrade. Not again. She really didn't enjoy looking after her sister's children. Oh, it might get better when they were older, and she could talk to them, and they could answer back. Have a conversation. She loved her niece and nephew, but babies bored her. So much mess and crying. Sarah preferred older children, who could come riding and skating with her.

"Do I have to?" she sighed, looking back at her mother.

"*Jah*," her mother answered. "You really do. I must finish my quilts for the sale, and Katie is busy, as well. It won't be for long, but you will have to get there early."

"Alright." Sarah continued up the stairs, not looking back again. Her mother watched her for a moment, then sighed heavily and went back into the kitchen.

Sarah collapsed across her bed. Another tedious day of child minding, when all she wanted to do was ride. It was such lovely weather; there was nothing she loved more in the world, than racing across the plains on Racer. He enjoyed it, too. Tomorrow was supposed to be wonderful, and now she would be cooped up inside her sister's house, trying to entertain a nine-month-old and a toddler.

Suddenly, the vision of the man on the plain today flashed through her mind. John Miller. He had looked at her like she was something from another world. Disapproving, as everyone was; Sarah had seen the sour look on his face. It was disappointing. She had thought that because he was new to the district, he might have an open mind. But all he saw was a girl on a horse, riding too fast, with a crooked prayer *kapps* and dislodged hair.

A pity. He was very handsome. Tall, with dark hair. Intriguing. Sarah mulled the vision of him over in her mind.

***

"Sarah, make sure you get into those corners," her mother said, depositing the bucket and mop at her feet. Then she walked out of the kitchen.

Sarah sighed dramatically, staring at the bucket. Tedious chores, before the day had even begun. Not that there was much to look forward to, anyway. Just babysitting.

She put the mop into the bucket, then slopped water on the floor, spreading it around disinterestedly. She didn't care what her mother said; there was no way she was moving stuff around. A quick going over with it, and then she was out of here.

Sarah hated housework, even more than babysitting, and that was saying something. Why couldn't she just be free to ride all day, the wind in her face, feeling the ground thunder beneath Racer's hooves?

At last. Mopping done, Sarah rushed out of the house, heading toward the stables. He would be getting restless. He always enjoyed a morning talk, even if she wasn't able to ride out. Racer. He had been her horse since she was twelve years old, and she liked him better than anyone.

She saddled him up, talking to him as she did so. "Not a long ride today, Racer," she said. "More's the pity. We have to head to Rebecca's to look after the babies." Racer looked at her with his deep brown eyes, seeming to sense the sorrow in her. He nudged her gently.

She was just about to head out, when her mother stopped her. "I don't want to hear any reports from people about you," she said, looking up at Sarah in the saddle. "No wild rides. Straight to your sister's house, young lady."

Sarah rolled her eyes. "Of course," she said. She picked up the reins, spurring Racer out of the stable.

It was a beautiful day, just as she had known it would be. Wildflowers bloomed everywhere; the trees swayed in the distance. Sarah stopped, breathing in the scent. She just felt more alive, somehow, out in nature. It was unnatural to be cooped up inside, tending babies and doing eternal housework. How did most women deal with it, after they were married?

She would never marry, she decided suddenly. At least, then, she wouldn't have to be a slave to a man and the children that would inevitably come. But the alternative didn't really appeal to her, either: being a spinster maid, living with her parents forever, at her mother's beck and call. What to do?

She wouldn't think about it, at all. She would just enjoy the ride. She spurred Racer on, heading across the plains towards her sister's farmhouse.

The wind felt so good. Surely one little ride, where she let Racer stretch his legs, couldn't hurt? She would still be able to get to Rebecca's on time.

Decision made, she spurred him on, flying across the plain. Freedom. A wide smile spread across her face, lodging there. There was no better feeling in the world.

The world whizzed past her, blurring. Racer picked up speed.

Suddenly, he stopped, rearing up. What was it? She barely had time to see the snake, as she flew over the horse's head, landing with a thud on the ground.

She sat up, slowly. The world was spinning. Had she knocked her head? She tried to get up, but it was all too much. She had to sit back down again.

"Are you alright?"

She jumped, almost leaping out of her skin. A figure in black loomed over her. She squinted, trying to make out who it was. Where on earth had they materialised from? She hadn't seen anyone on the plain, not even in the distance.

Then, she knew. She remembered. It was the man she had seen yesterday, John Miller.

"*Jah*, I think so," she said ruefully, rubbing her head. "I don't know what happened."

"A snake is what happened," John said. "I saw it as I was running over to you."

"A snake?" Sarah wrinkled up her nose. "But it's too early for them."

"It's because of the warm weather we've been having," he said. "They come out earlier." He crouched down, looking at her. "You were very lucky. I saw you go clear over your horse's head. Have you any injuries?"

Sarah tried to concentrate on his voice. But the sight of him, crouching down close to her, made her catch her breath. She had been right. He was a very handsome man, and she was enjoying the look of concern that was in his face as he stared at her.

"I think so," she said, gingerly. Maybe he would carry her in his arms? The thought made her glow, for a moment. Then she shook her head at her own muddled thinking.

"Try to stand up," he said. She did so, feeling woozy. But at least she was on her feet, which was something.

"Where were you going?" John asked now, reaching out to steady her. The touch of his hand on hers made her heart thump. What on earth was happening to her? It must be because of the fall. It had addled her wits, temporarily.

"To my sister's," she answered. It seemed so long ago that she had set out for Rebecca's. Was she late? That was all she needed. Rebecca would complain to their mother, and she would never hear the end of it.

"Do you want me to help you get there?" he asked, frowning. "Or do you want to go home?"

Sarah grimaced. If she headed home, her mother would scold her all day about her recklessness. No, better to push on to Rebecca's. At least, then, she could salvage the situation. A little.

"I need to get there," she said, starting to walk. She turned back to look at him. "Why are you out here?"

He blushed, slightly. Why, she didn't know. "I was just going for a walk," he said, slowly. Why wouldn't he meet her eyes? It was like he wasn't telling her the truth. But why would that be? She shook her head, slightly. She was being fanciful, again.

She went up to Racer, grabbing his reins, talking to him soothingly. Then she put her foot in the stirrup.

"What are you doing?" John approached her quickly. "You can't ride. You've had a nasty fall. I will walk with you. We can lead the horse."

Sarah turned to him, astonished. "But I will be late," she said, gritting her teeth. "And I am perfectly fine!"

"Why are you so stubborn?" he said, frowning at her. "Your sister will understand why you are late when we explain it to her."

Sarah shook her head. She was appalled to find tears had sprung into her eyes. "You don't understand," she said, bitterly. "She will know why I fell, and so why I am late, and then she will start scolding me, as everyone does!" A single tear fell down on her cheek. Oh, this was so frustrating! She wasn't one of those girls who cried at the drop of a hat. She rarely cried over anything. Why then, did she feel as if she were about start sobbing like silly Grace Fisher, the cry baby back at school?

John leant over, stroking her arm. She looked up at him, appalled to see sympathy in his eyes. Yes, he was feeling sorry for her. He must think she was like all the other girls he had ever met.

"Sarah, it's alright," he said, soothingly.

"How do you know my name?" she said, sniffling. "I never told you yesterday."

John started. "I told my family about you, when I eventually got home," he said, carefully.

Sarah's eyes widened. "Oh, I see," she said, in a disappointed voice. "Of course. Everyone has heard of me, even people who are new to the district. Silly Sarah Glick, who rides her horse too fast, dislikes babies and hates housework."

John smiled. "Well, I didn't know you hated housework," he said. He stared at her, his eyes glowing. Sarah felt her breath stop, again.

"Why does everyone disapprove of me?" she burst out, gazing at John. As if she expected an answer! He would just start lecturing her, the same as everyone else. He had done so, yesterday. She was so used to it she barely noticed it anymore.

"I suppose," he said, slowly, "because you are different to the other girls in our faith. People want everyone to be the same, and feel the same."

Sarah gasped. "*Jah*," she breathed. "That is so true!" She felt sorry for herself. She was a duckling in a swan's nest, there was no doubt about it. Did this John understand that? He seemed to.

"I think you are wonderful," he blurted, gazing at her. "But you should be careful with your riding. I would hate to see you get hurt."

"You think I am wonderful?" Sarah breathed. She gazed at him. Maybe he wasn't like all the others.

But then, he had told her to be careful, as well. And was that a slight frown on his face?

"You can escort me to my sisters," she said, stiffly. "Thank you for coming to my service. I appreciate it."

She started walking off, leading Racer.

She didn't see the look of longing that John Miller gave her, as he slowly followed her.

***

Her sister was down the steps of her veranda as soon as they arrived.

"Sarah! Where on earth have you been? You are over an hour late!" Rebecca had her hands on her hips, frowning.

Sarah shrugged. "I fell off Racer," she said. "John helped me."

"You fell off Racer?" Rebecca repeated. "Are you hurt?"

Sarah shrugged, again. "I feel well, I think," she said. She handed Racer's reins to John. "Would you be able to take him to the stable for me? It's just around the back."

"Certainly," said John, taking the reins. He looked at her for a moment, then led the horse away.

Rebecca gazed after him. "Who is he?" she whispered. "I don't think I have ever seen him before."

"His name is John Miller," answered Sarah. "He has just moved here with his family."

Rebecca gazed at her, her eyes wide. "And he just happened along, after your fall?"

"*Jah*," Sarah said. "He was out walking. I bumped into him yesterday, as well."

They started walking up the farmhouse steps. "I think that young man likes you, Sarah," Rebecca whispered.

Sarah stopped. "What are you talking about? He just happened along, and was nice enough to assist me."

Rebecca smiled. "I can tell, by the way he looks at you," she said. She narrowed her eyes, looking over her sister. "It's good that you look decent today, even though you had a fall. I have seen you with your hair out, and your *kapps* dislodged. Dirt on your apron. At least you are looking better than usual."

Sarah felt stung. "You are too concerned with appearances, sister," she said, primly. "And as for any interest from that young man, you are imagining it. Besides, I never want to court anyone. I don't want to marry, and get stuck in a farmhouse being a slave, tending to screaming babies forever."

Rebecca looked at her as if she had lost her mind. "There is more to it than that, little sister," she said sharply. "What about love – for your husband, and your children? To serve those you love is a blessing. I couldn't imagine life without my family."

"I'm not criticising you..."

"Enough." Rebecca put a hand in the air to silence her. "You are young, and foolish. I hope that you will see the error of your ways before it is too late, Sarah. For you just might find life passes you by, and suddenly you are a spinster dreaming of what could have been." She walked ahead into the house.

Sarah frowned. Rebecca was just justifying her choices, wasn't she? Not that there were many, really. If you belonged to the community, you always ended up being a wife and mother. Love. Sarah scoffed. Was so called love worth all the nonsense attached to it? Nothing had led her to believe so, thus far.

And yet. She remembered how she had felt, when John had helped her up. The fission of attraction. But what did it matter, anyway? John would prove himself like all the rest of them. Wanting to change her.

Here he was, now. Walking toward her. Her heart started beating faster.

"Sarah." He bowed, his dark eyes shining. She looked at him, awkwardly. What should she say? Should she invite him inside, for a drink? It would probably be polite. After all, he had helped her today.

"Would you like a glass of water, or a coffee?" She blushed, slightly.

"No, no," he said. "I should get going. Chores to do." And yet he stood there, still looking at her.

"Well," Sarah looked at the ground. "Thank you for helping me today. I really appreciated it."

"My pleasure," he said. He looked at her, almost beseechingly. Then he abruptly turned on his heel, and walked away. Back up the track.

Sarah watched him go. She was feeling odd. Was John Miller a friend, or a critic? Was she being judged by him?

She simply didn't know. She only knew that she wanted him to come back. To be by her side. For just a little bit longer.

***

John walked briskly. He was going to be in trouble with his father, again. He didn't even know why he had decided to walk across the plain this morning. He had many chores to do, and his father knew how long each one took. He would be at the farm, now, wondering where on earth John had disappeared to.

He frowned. He was only being half truthful with himself. He knew why he had suddenly decided on the morning walk. He had been hoping to see Sarah again.

He hadn't been able to stop thinking about her. It was as simple as that. He knew that she was considered wild by the community. He knew everyone thought that she wasn't marriage material, that she was too forthright, and reckless. He had seen the evidence of that recklessness, not once, but twice. Yesterday, when she had almost run him down with her horse. And today, when she had fallen from it.

He thought her reckless, like everybody else. And yet, there was something so charismatic about her. The vision of the girl on the horse, hair flying and eyes glittering, was enchanting. And the fact that she had the strength of will to be herself, in the face of disapproval.

But she had admitted it, today. She hated housework, and didn't like babies. How could he sensibly try to court a young woman who had no desire to set up a home and have a family, as was the done thing in their faith? John was a conventional man. He wanted a home and family of his own; he wanted to have children. How could he court a girl who expressed her disdain for both?

He thought of Miriam, the girl he had been courting. Meek Miriam, whose sole desire in life was marriage and children. She was the type of woman he should be considering, not a wild girl like Sarah who flouted convention.

He sighed, deeply. He had better get moving. Sarah would probably not agree to courting him, anyway, with her beliefs. If he suggested it to her, she would probably laugh in his face.

Best to forget all about her. With a nod of decision, John set off towards his farm.

***

The babies were screaming. Sarah had a thudding headache. She didn't know if it was a leftover from her fall today, or just the children. Maybe a combination of both.

Would they ever stop? She had tried everything. Fed them, changed them, tried to get them to sleep. But still, they carried on. She juggled little Eli, the nine-month-old, on her hip, desperately looking down the track to see if Rebecca's buggy was on the way. Samuel, the toddler, had his arms wrapped around her legs, bawling like a banshee.

"Your Mamm will be home soon," she said, in a false cheery voice. "Let's sit on the sofa with a picture book."

She walked into the living room, picking up a book. It was one of her own favorites from childhood. She settled down on the sofa, getting Samuel to crawl up beside her. She kept Eli on her lap.

It was difficult, juggling the book and the baby, but she managed to get it open. And then she started reading.

It was such a sweet story, and she got lost in it, just a little bit. The children quietened down as she read. She could feel Eli's head starting to loll. Samuel snuggled up closer, his eyes riveted onto the book.

As she read the last page, she was amazed to see that Eli had fallen asleep. And Samuel was almost there. He burrowed his head into her side, kissing her.

Her heart melted, just a little bit. She looked at him, being very careful that she didn't disturb Eli.

"Did you like that story, little one?" she whispered. Samuel looked up at her, his big blue eyes shining. He nodded.

"Sa-rah," he said, stringing out her name, as he always did. "I love you."

Sarah gasped. He had never said those words to her, before.

"I love you, too, Samuel," she whispered, leaning over to kiss him on the head. He sighed contentedly, before his eyelids started fluttering and finally closed. He was asleep.

Sarah closed the book. It hadn't been easy, but she had got there. They had settled down. Reading the book had been the trick. Even when they had kept crying, she had continued. Her calm determination had soothed them.

Was that the trick, with babies? Being calm? Not getting upset when they cried?

She knew in her heart that it wasn't always that simple. She had seen Rebecca, the calmest person she knew, sometimes unable to settle them. But it did seem to help. And it made her feel better able to cope with them, if she was feeling calm, instead of stressed and anxious.

And how sweet that moment had been, when little Samuel had told her he loved her.

The front door opened. It was Caleb, Rebecca's husband. She looked at him, raising a finger to her mouth to signal to be quiet. Caleb smiled, walking quietly into the living room.

"Well, well," he whispered. "What do we have here? Well done, Sarah."

Sarah glowed. Usually, whenever Caleb walked into the house when she was looking after the children, it was bedlam. He would have to take over, settling the babies, and Sarah, frazzled, would look for her escape.

They both turned as they heard the buggy pull up outside. And then, Rebecca walked into the room. She raised her eyebrows in amazement at the calm scene in front of her.

"Sarah," she whispered. "What has happened? Where is my hot headed little sister?"

Sarah smiled. Rebecca gently eased Eli out of her arms, carrying him to his cot. Caleb did the same with Samuel, making cooing sounds to the little boy as he stirred in his arms.

Sarah watched her sister and brother-in-law meet in the hallway, after putting their children down. Caleb rested a hand on Rebecca's arm, and she gazed up at him with such a look of love that Sarah gasped.

She had to turn her head away from the tender scene, blinking back tears. Why was she so overcome with emotion? It was inexplicable.

As she said good bye to them, she couldn't resist poking her head into the children's bedrooms, watching them sleep. They looked so precious. Her heart overflowed with love for them.

She rode Racer over the plain, heading home. For once, she listened to the voice in her head that said to not go too fast. She didn't feel the need. And she was half hoping that she might spot John Miller, walking.

But she didn't see him. Why did she feel so disappointed? She barely knew the man, after all.

And he would never deign to court her. Her reputation preceded her, and he was a solemn man. Even though his eyes shone when he beheld her. Sarah shivered, picturing them in her mind.

John's dark eyes followed her all the way home, over the plain.

***

A week passed. Sarah rode out over the plain, but she didn't see him. She tried to tell herself it was for the best. She told herself that he was too solemn for her; they wouldn't have been a good match.

But still, her heart yearned to see him. Her heart would jump when she would see a figure in the distance, her eyes deceiving her. It was him! But it never was. He had obviously decided that she was too hard work.

Today was a magical spring day, a hint of summer in the air. She had ridden Racer a bit, but not too fast. Maybe her fall had made her more cautious, she had no idea. But suddenly, she was aware that her beloved horse could be injured by her recklessness. It just didn't seem worth it, anymore.

She bent down to pick some wildflowers. She thought of the bible passage that she had read last night. It had made her stop and ponder. It was Proverbs 14:16, which said, "One who is wise is cautious and turns away from evil, but a fool is reckless and careless." Had that been her? Had she smashed through life, careless of what was before her? She didn't think that she was a fool. She wanted to be wise.

Suddenly, she looked up. Was it really him, on the horizon? John Miller? Her heart started thumping, uncomfortably.

It was. He walked slowly toward her, his face solemn. And then, he was standing there.

"I thought it was you," he said, his eyes shining. He looked down at the ground, as if he didn't know what to say further.

"John," Sarah said, staring at him. She took a deep breath. It was now, or never.

"*Jah*?" He looked up at her. His face told her all she needed to know.

"I'm sorry," she whispered. "I realise now that I have been reckless. I want to change."

"What?" He looked like he couldn't believe what she had just said.

"Oh, I will probably never be meek," she admitted. "I have a temper. But I have learnt that I should try to control it, and remain calm. I want to be a better person."

He looked at her in amazement. "Sarah," he said. "I love you. For who you are. I wouldn't want you to change. I like that you are different from the other girls." He blushed. "Maybe just tone it down, a little."

"You love me?" she whispered. Her heart overflowed with gladness. "John, I love you, too!"

He stared at her, as if he had never heard such good news. He gently approached her. She gazed up at him, her heart overflowing.

"So, I may court you?" he whispered. "And one day we might marry? Even though you hate housework and don't like babies?"

She laughed, gently. "I mightn't ever like housework," she admitted. "But I know it is a necessary part of life. As for babies – well, maybe one day?" She looked at him, blushing.

He smiled. "Maybe one day," he said. "We can have a long engagement, and wait until you feel you are ready. I don't mind waiting."

Sarah breathed a sigh of relief, and gratitude. It was simply astonishing. A man who was willing to give her the space she needed, and loved her for herself, despite her faults. Who was willing to not listen to everything that he had heard, but simply judge her on what he saw.

That was a man worth keeping. She finally understood what this love thing was all about.

THE END

AN AMISH WINTER

TERRI DOWNES

Summer, 1905

The air was finally beginning to clear. Somewhere overhead, a bird began to sing, as though assuring the world it remained unmoved by present circumstances.

"Are you leaving with the others?" Jacob asked.

Mary looked down at her hands, twisted in her lap. "My family want to go," she said.

"I don't blame them," said Jacob. "But do you?"

"How could I stay without them?" asked Mary quietly.

Jacob was silent for a minute.

"You know what I would suggest – what I would ask," he said.

Mary did not reply. She knew.

"I know that, after everything, you may have trouble..." Jacob paused. "Trusting."

Mary leaned back, taking her weight on her hands, feeling the dry grass beneath them. She nodded, as though only to herself. Jacob looked at her, his expression indescribably sad.

"I'm so sorry," he said. "About everything. Everything you've been through. But I hope – I have to hope, and I have to ask now, while I can – "

The bird stopped singing.

"Do you trust me?" he asked. "Could you... trust me?"

***

Two months earlier

"Mary, are you listening?"

"What?"

Mary tilted her head towards her brother, though she did not look up from the furrowed piece of ground that she had been staring at as though she were preparing to interrogate it.

"I said we should be getting at least five bushels per acre," said Paul, waving his arms expansively as he indicated the field before them. "I knew *daed* was on to something with this winter wheat. I bet everyone else is wishing they had joined in when he suggested combining resources for the first year."

"Some of them did," Mary pointed out, scuffling at the ground with the toe of her boot. "The Kauffmans and the Yoders have those few acres on the eastern side, by the windmill. Everyone else is focused on their cattle raising."

"More fool them," said Paul. "If it doesn't rain soon they're going to have problems – meanwhile we're nearly ready to harvest. And the windmill's finished just in time, too."

He nodded to himself. Mary was not sure whether it was her irritable frame of mind causing her to be unfair, but she thought he looked a little smug. He, and their eldest brother Albert, and their father, had all been looking a little too smug ever since they had started construction on that windmill.

They had only arrived in Iowa in September, along with twenty-one other Plain families who had all moved over from Pennsylvania, arriving over the course of a few months. Many had been from their old community. Most of the families had settled themselves with cattle ranges, breeding from the stock they had brought with them across the country. Mary's father had had a different plan. As soon as they had arrived, he had busied himself with buying up vast areas of fertile land and planting it with winter wheat. Albert had expressed his concerns over whether they would be able to plant in time, as they only got everything sorted by the beginning of winter when the temperature was beginning to drop. But a slightly delayed first frost and perfect winter conditions meant that now, coming up to Summer, they were looking forward to a bumper crop of wheat, and did not have to join in the worries of their neighbors over the recent lack of rain.

"Daed was right," reaffirmed Paul happily as they started to make for home, the small white farmstead in the middle of the plain, distinguishable from any other houses within view by the tall shape of the windmill standing near it. "The risk was worth it, all the loans, everything. We'll pay them back in no time."

The loans.

Mary could not help but glance sceptically at her brother as they walked. Did he know? Had her father told him? Or had it been a secret between him and –

"Samuel!" called Paul suddenly.

Mary stopped short, feeling for a moment as though Paul had pulled the name from her head. Then she focused her thoughts and realized that Paul was waving at two figures cutting across the pasture to their right.

"Jacob!"

Paul waved at the two men as they approached. He sent a smile in Mary's direction, which Mary felt herself obliged to return. He would of course expect her to be pleased to see Samuel, and she did not want to give her feelings away. Not yet.

"Evening," said Samuel, as he and Jacob came onto the path alongside Mary and Paul.

Jacob smiled in greeting. He and Samuel, both young and unmarried, had become good friends on the long journey to Iowa, and now went nearly everywhere together. One might have thought they were brothers, if not for the fact that they looked nothing alike. Where Samuel was fair, with corn colored hair and light blue eyes, Jacob's complexion was muddy, his hair a dingy red.Where Samuel was strong and well-built, Jacob was lean, looking as though he had grown too tall for his strength. He carried himself as though he had just woken up, as though he were waiting to stretch.

Samuel had been the most handsome man Mary had ever met, she had known so as soon as she had seen him at their first gathering before the big move. His bearing and manner seemed to carry the assumption that people would look at him – but he had looked at Mary, at that first meeting, and smiled.

He was smiling now. Mary looked away.

She was determined to act normally, but she was having trouble collecting her wits as Samuel fell into step alongside her. As though they were already engaged, as though everything had been settled. She felt him looking at her – could he tell that she knew?

"I haven't seen you in a few days," he said, softly enough that it was obvious he was speaking only to her, but loud enough that the others could hear. Mary blushed. He really was being far too obvious – wasn't he? Maybe they did things differently in his old community, but in hers, courtships were quiet things.

"Did you two know how well the wheat is doing?" she said, deliberately catching Paul's eye and smiling as she spoke, which she knew would set him off. It did.

"Oh yes," he said excitedly. "Five bushels an acre at least!"

He started explaining the plans they had for harvest, and how they had been working to get the mill ready so they could grind the flour themselves.

"Will you be selling us your crop to grind, Jacob?" he asked. Jacob's family, the Yoders, had been one of the only two families to take Mary's father up on his offer of land and seeds. They had only planted a couple of acres, on the edge of the land Mary's father had bought, but they would surely benefit from the success of the wheat.

Jacob smiled in that way he had, as though he was thinking of something privately funny. "Maybe," he said. "I wasn't sure whether I should keep the whole crop or burn some of it so I can use the space for corn."

"Corn?" exclaimed Paul, with the attitude of a man who had been farming for decades and knew everything there was to know about the subject. "You'd need a miracle to grow corn in this weather. You're much better off keeping the wheat and letting us grind it. The windmill's nearly done, you know."

Mary was starting to feel embarrassed. As pleased as she had been to find their family settled and prospering so soon, this attitude of her brothers and father seemed too close to pride to allow her much comfort.

"I heard," Jacob was saying.

"We were actually headed over to take a look if we could," said Samuel.

Paul nodded, and seemed about to launch into a description of the brand new windmill, but Mary spoke first.

"You can't," she said.

The boys all glanced at her.

"Why not?" demanded Paul.

"It's getting dark."

"What's that got to do with anything?"

"Weren't you listening to *daed*?" Mary felt her tone becoming sharp, and tried to sound more indulgent. "You can't take a candle or a lantern into the mill."

"Oh, right..." Paul looked a little crestfallen.

"Why?" asked Jacob, still smiling.

"It's the flour dust in the air," explained Mary. "It can catch fire."

"Flour catches fire?" he said, sounding intrigued. "I didn't know that."

"Not by itself so much, not when it's in a sack or a bowl. It's only when it's floating in the air, I think because the fire can get to all the little pieces individually..."

"I never knew," said Jacob. "Did you know that, Samuel?"

"Of course," said Samuel, who had been giving sidelong glances to Mary as she had been speaking. Rather than expounding on the topic, however, he changed the subject.

Mary was again unsure of whether she was simply in a more suspicious frame of mind than usual, but she was certain, as she looked at Samuel, that he had not known. That he was lying to seem clever.

This was going to be a problem, she realized. How could she go courting with a man whom she could not trust?

And even Jacob and Paul, walking along and listening to Samuel – Mary kept looking at them, and wondering – *did you know, too? How many people knew about this before I did?*

Mary clenched and unclenched her fists as they walked. Something would need to be done.

***

"How did you find out?" asked Mary's mother, her brow creased.

"Mrs. Yoder mentioned it," said Mary. "In passing. Though – forgive me – but I can't see that that's the most important point here. When were *you* going to tell me?"

Mary's mother hesitated, and glanced at her father. He was standing at the window of their front room, staring out across the yard and the space beyond, towards his new windmill.

"We – well, we thought – " began her mother.

"We thought we would wait until you had had a chance to get to know Samuel," said her father, turning from the window and facing his daughter. His expression was calm and earnest. "You were getting on so well with him, we thought it might make you uncomfortable to know that he was the one who lent us the wheat money."

Mary frowned a little, turning this over in her mind.

"Yes," she said, "but *he* knew that he had lent the money. He had information I didn't..."

"Goodness, Mary, you're not negotiating a business deal," laughed her father.

"It's not as though *you* owe him anything," said her mother.

"Yes, I know that..." said Mary slowly, hesitating.

She was having trouble remembering her original objections. She had been deeply shocked when Jacob's mother had casually referred to the loan Samuel had given to her father, the one that had allowed him to get the crop planted in time, the success of which had then enabled him to secure a second loan for the construction of the windmill.

She had immediately thought back to the way that Samuel had approached her that night he had first invited her out for a drive. He had been smiling, the way he always did, with that calm assurance that she had so often admired. But had he been so assured because he felt that she did, in fact, owe him something for her family's success?

There were so many questions she wanted to ask. When had her father first asked Samuel about the loan? Had it been before or after Samuel had started smiling at Mary, seeking her out and engaging her in conversation? Had it been Samuel's idea not to tell Mary, or her father's?

And had her parents' encouragement of her courtship with Samuel been because they thought the two of them were well suited, or because they felt obliged to the man?

But now, looking at the reassuring smile her father was showing her, Mary could not bring herself to ask. It might sound as though she was accusing them of – what?

So she nodded. "I understand," she said. "I just feel foolish, acting in ignorance."

"We're sorry that you feel that way," her father said kindly. "It wasn't our intention."

Mary told him that she understood, and agreed that they would not mention her knowledge to Samuel just yet. Then she excused herself, saying that she had to see to her chores.

When she walked outside into the front yard, she found her gaze drawn to the windmill. It soared up against the sky, its four sailcloths giving the unsettling impression of outstretched arms. With the sun setting behind it, all she could see was its shape in shadow.

***

Mary could not think of a real reason why she should drop her courtship with Samuel. The points her father had made were sensible, and the liking she had felt for Samuel was genuine. Perhaps secrecy really had been the best thing, she considered, else she might have been confused as to whether her feeling had sprung from gratitude or from real admiration.

Yet, she found herself avoiding Samuel. Not entirely – they still went for rides, and walks. But she never asked when they would see each other again. She never pushed for extra time together, or told him that she had missed him.

He did not seem to notice the change. Mary tried to convince herself that this was simply because he was confident that she liked him, and not because he did not care whether she did or not. She tried not to count the number of times he actually asked for her opinion.

She spent the afternoons before their scheduled drives going over potential topics of conversation, trying to talk herself into feeling more comfortable than she did by pre-planning the time they would have together.

On one such afternoon, as the sun was sinking over the wide plains in a haze of orange, she was so far gone in her thoughts as she completed her chores in readiness for her evening out that she failed to notice Jacob approaching across the back yard until he was level with the porch. When she saw his long sunset-cast shadow fall across the steps she jumped, sending a puff of flour into the air.

"It's only me," said Jacob, holding his hands up in front of him, his shoulders in their slightly relaxed slouch like always. "Are you all right?"

"Fine," said Mary, placing a hand to her heart, then pulling it away and glancing down in irritation when she saw that she had smeared flour on the neck of her dress.

Jacob watched her, one side of his mouth quirked in a partial smile. Mary shook her head at her thoughtlessness and smiled back.

Something about the openness of his expression made her feel more calm than she had in weeks – since learning of the loan.

"I'm just here to arrange getting my grain milled," said Jacob, walking up the steps. "Your father's agreed to buy my crop. Seems funny, seeing as how I bought the seeds from him in the first place, but we'll all profit in the end, I'm sure."

"You're not going to try corn, then?" asked Mary.

"Not with the weather the way it is."

They had had barely any rain in the last month, and the almanacs were predicting a very dry summer.

"Maybe you could try next year," said Mary. "Or you could alternate the wheat with a legume crop."

"That's a good idea," said Jacob thoughtfully. "And I'm trying to think of ways around the water problem."

"Like what?" asked Mary. It felt good, she realized, to be speaking like this. Discussing important, practical things, things that would reward you for the thought you put into them, instead of winding your concentration around ideas like love and betrayal and gratitude.

"Irrigation, maybe. There's a brook running alongside the my land, between mine and the Kauffman's, you know, and I thought I could use it for the fields. It's still flowing, even without the rain."

"I know the one you mean," said Mary. "I think it's ground water, from a spring, so you don't have to worry about the rain. Will the Kauffmans do the same on their side?"

"John's still ill," said Jacob, shaking his head. "And the oldest boys are having trouble handling things on their own."

"Perhaps you could do it for them," said Mary.

Jacob considered this, and smiled. "Of course," he said. "I should have thought of that."

"I'm sure you would have," Mary assured him. Although she wanted to keep talking, she knew that Samuel would be coming by soon, so she turned her attention back to the table in front of her.

"What are you doing?" asked Jacob, not moving.

"Kneading dough," said Mary, raising an eyebrow.

Jacob laughed. "No, I can see that, I just wondered why you were doing it out here on the porch."

"It gets too hot in the kitchen at this time," shrugged Mary. "We still need to put up shutters to block the afternoon light, but the boys are all busy getting ready for the harvest."

"Ah. I thought you might be using the sunlight instead of a lamp in case you set fire to the flour," he teased.

Mary rolled her eyes. "Only if you throw the flour over the lamp," she said.

"I'll have to try that sometime," Jacob said. "I keep trying to imagine what you were describing, but it's difficult."

"Hmm..." Mary glanced at her kneading. She was just about done. "Hold on."

She went back into the kitchen and came out with a candle in a holder, along with a bowl of water. She handed Jacob the bowl, then set the candle on the far end of the table and lit it.

"Right," she said. "This looks better at night, but for once there's no breeze, so I might as well show you now. Have the water ready in case I make a mistake."

Jacob nodded eagerly, looking for all the world like a schoolboy. Mary could not help but smile at his expression. She took a small handful of flour, then stood at arm's length away from the candle and cast the flour carefully over the flame.

A ball of fire blossomed out from the candle, reaching up and engulfing the falling flour in a flash of light which disappeared into a wisp of yellow flame.

It lasted only a second, but left an after image of light burning in Mary's eyes, forming a bright haze around Jacob's face as she looked up at him to gauge his expression. He looked completely entranced.

"That was amazing! Can we do it again?"

"One's enough," said Mary. "Getting overexcited is how accidents happen."

"All right," he said reluctantly. "Then – "

"What are you doing?" a voice called from across the yard.

Mary and Jacob turned to see Samuel striding toward them. He did not look pleased.

"I was just showing Jacob how the fire reacts with the flour..." began Mary, but she trailed off as Samuel's face remained set in a scowl.

"I asked to see," said Jacob, keeping his voice light. He glanced at Mary. As she met his gaze, she shook her head slightly, indicating that he did not need to stay and defend her. He hesitated for a moment, then said, "Well, I'd best catch your father before he heads off."

Jacob disappeared into the house. Mary tried to smile at Samuel, but she was thrown by his still-angry expression.

****

The next day, Mary sought out her parents once more. She had spent half the night thinking about the decision she had to make, but it was getting harder and harder to ignore the way her heart was turning.

She felt as though she had been caught up, off her feet, for the months she and Samuel had been courting. Caught up by his good looks, by his confidence, by the fact that he seemed to favor her over any other girl in their new community. Even the fact that he had come from a different community within Lancaster had added to his appeal; unlike young men such as Jacob, Mary had not ever known Samuel as a boy, but only as a man.

It had taken the shock of finding out about the loan to shake her from her trance. She had started having doubts – and then, with her newly opened eyes, finding more things to doubt about. She had started to notice how little they ever spoke about her, the two of them. It was always Samuel leading the conversation, and Mary trying to show him how interested she was.

And yesterday... he had gone on about her candle trick for almost half of the buggy ride they had taken. "It's not safe, you were just showing off, think about how you'd behave if you were running a home," and on and on.

Mary had tried to explain that she had done it before, and had even apologized, admitting that it had not been the most sensible thing to do. But he had not let up. And eventually, Mary had started to wonder... was it what she had done that had annoyed him? Or the fact that she had done it for Jacob?

She had thought about how happy Jacob always was to see her, how he sought her smiles and opinion... how friendly they had been back in Lancaster, and how she barely saw him these days, since she had been seeing Samuel. And she had wondered.

She left this latter concern unspoken to her parents, as she could not be sure of Jacob's feelings for her, or Samuel's feelings about those feelings, but she explained that she had misgivings about Samuel's character.

She had been nervous about broaching the subject, as her parents had both been so pleased by Samuel's courtship, but they both sat and listened to her speak without interrupting. In fact, Mary watched her father nodding thoughtfully and began to think how good it was of him not to object to this, given what he owed Samuel and how careful he was bound to be not to offend him. She was going to say as much – but her father spoke first.

"Now, Mary... are you sure that you are not reacting too strongly?" he asked.

Mary looked at him.

"You don't want to make a mistake," he said. "Are you sure you've thought this through?"

His voice was calm, his expression kind. His eyebrows were raised.

As though he knew better than her. As thought he knew that she was simply being over emotional, and that she did not know her own mind.

Mary felt something cold spreading at the bottom of her chest.

"I'm quite sure," she said, keeping her voice steady, even as fear began to make itself known. He could not have misunderstood what she had been saying. So why was he questioning her?

He had always trusted her in the past. Always. He knew that she respected his authority, and had never challenged her unnecessarily over the fact. He had always told her how proud he was of her intelligence, and how she could work things out on her own.

Surely he would not...

But he did.

"Well, I would rather you allowed Samuel to go on courting you," he said. "For now. Something might change, you know. You might realize you were wrong."

Mary spoke quietly. "I don't think I will, *daed*."

Her father's expression closed. "Well, I want you to try," he said. And nodded, sharply. And then left the room.

Mary turned to her mother – who was already turning away.

"*Mamme*?" she said.

"Trust your *daed*," her mother said. "He knows what's best."

Mary left the room without another word.

***

"What's the problem?" asked Albert. "If you don't like him, break it off."

He grabbed the side of the bin in front of him and gave it a shake. "This one's secure!" he called up to Paul on the next floor. "Try the hopper."

"Which one's the hopper?" Paul yelled down.

"Where you put the grain in," Albert yelled back. "You'd think with how excited he is about this, he'd remember what everything's called," he commented to Mary.

He and Paul were double checking the workings of the windmill before they started the harvest. They had already checked the sailcloths; the shafts, pinions and spindles; and the two huge stone millwheels.

"That's what I wanted to do," said Mary, "but *daed* thinks I'm making a mistake."

She did not tell him the shadowed suspicions in her heart, that their father was insisting she keep Samuel happy because of what they owed him. She did not want to sully her father's image in the eyes of his sons; nor, indeed, did she want Albert to become angry at her for suggesting such a thing.

"Hopper's fine," said Paul, as his feet appeared on the ladder above their heads.

"Well then, either you're wrong or *daed's* wrong," said Albert.

He led the way back outside, into bright sunshine that made Mary squint. The sun was still relentless, the sky obstinately blue, the air baked to a crisp every single morning. Many of the families in the area were beginning to wonder what they would do if the rain continued to stay away,

"Right," said Paul, following them out. "You'll find out soon enough."

He looked back up at the windmill. "A lot of people are going to be buying our flour," he said. "Especially now they haven't been able to plant much themselves."

"It's a shame," said Albert, not sounding too concerned. "It's turning into a real drought now, I don't know how everyone's going to manage. I think we'll be the only ones around here who'll have had any success this year."

Mary felt herself becoming desperate. If only they were not all so caught up in this wretched windmill business. She could not remember any of her family being so distant and unfeeling as this before. She was beginning to wish that they had never even come here, that they had just stayed home in Lancaster. All this talk of crop yields and profits... it felt so wordly. Even though the windmill was approved technology, her father and brothers were so obsessed with the thing that Mary felt that they might as well have gone and bought one of those new motorcar things that everyone seemed to have had in the towns that they had passed through on their way here.

"Listen. It's just that I think *daed*... likes Samuel too much," she pressed on. "As a... friend. And I think he might not realize that were not suited."

Albert dragged his gaze away from the sailcloths, which were currently immobile as the mechanisms were all in place now and should not be turned when there was nothing to grind.

"And what do you want us to do about it?" he asked, as though conceding a huge favor.

Mary swallowed down her irritation. "Just... there are a few people who knew Samuel, from his community, back in Lancaster," she said. "Who knew his family. You're all working together in the harvest – just, if you could ask them, in passing, what they think of Samuel. What they know of him. Something."

Albert sighed. Mary turned to Paul. "Please," she repeated, hoping her younger brother would be a little softer.

Paul looked at Albert. "I don't mind," he said.

Mary took that as a yes.

***

She left things at that, for a little while. She did not have to think too much about seeing Samuel, or indeed her father or brothers, as they were all busy dawn til dusk with the harvest. And she kept herself as busy as possible, so that at least half the times Samuel tried to see her she could tell him that she was in the middle of something.

As the days passed, the ground remained dry, the plains wide and brown under the sun as though they had been scorched by it. The cattle farmers were beginning to become seriously worried. Some even began to speak of returning to Lancaster. Mary's father greeted this news with annoyance, and Mary could not help the uncharitable thought that he was angry not because he might lose his community, but because he might lose his customers.

She repented of the thought after she had had it, but it left its shadow behind.

When Samuel mentioned to her, one evening, that he had also been considering whether staying was the right option, Mary almost panicked, thinking that he meant to propose, that he wanted them to wed and return to Lancaster together. She quickly began to speak of the last dry summer she had experienced, when she was seven, and how everyone had felt then, but that the rain had come anyway, and that if they just remained faithful in prayer –

She realized, as she spoke, that Samuel was not really paying attention. She did not mind, as she was just trying to keep the subject changed. They were walking back to her home, and had almost reached the yard gate, and soon she could say good night.

As they reached the gate, she turned to say goodnight, hoping to cut off any ideas of him coming inside with her. But as she did so, she caught sight of something.

"Oh, look!" she cried excitedly, and pointed.

Over the long line of the horizon, a cloud was rising. Just one, by itself, but it was no wisp that would blow away in the night. It was large, substantial, and heavy, with a darkness underneath the pink caused by the setting sun that hinted at the possibility of rain. Rain, at last.

"It's a cloud!"

"I can see that," said Samuel, sounding a little amused.

Mary ignored him, looking out at the cloud with as much satisfaction as if she had made it herself. She hardly noticed Samuel beside her, looking away from it.

But then he glanced down at her. And as she reached out to open the gate, he reached out to stop her, placing a hand on the latch. And the other hand on the small of her back.

Mary felt a jolt up her spine, and stepped away with a jerk, turning so that her back was to the gate. She stared at Samuel. He looked quite calm – had she made a mistake? But he reached out again, to her shoulder, and ran his hand down to her elbow. His expression was soft, a smile playing on his lips. Mary almost wondered if her reaction was unwarranted.

But he was not – he was not supposed to do this. He was not allowed. Mary took a deep breath. Whether his old community had different rules or not – and, really, how different could they be, now that she thought about it – she had not given him permission to do this. They were not engaged. They were not married. He had no right to touch her.

She pulled her arm away. Samuel raised an eyebrow. It looked like a challenge.

What can I say? Mary wondered. *What can I say to make him leave? Please, please, leave –*

And then she heard them. Footsteps. Louder than they should have been, on the dust of the road, or perhaps that was because Mary was so happy to hear them.

"Jacob," she said, unable to keep the relief from her voice. She caught Samuel's frown, but did not care, as Jacob approached with his easy smile.

"Evening," he said, but Samuel was already turning around.

"Evening," he replied. "I have to go."

"Oh, all right – " Jacob hesitated as he found himself speaking to his friend's receding back.

It may have been Mary's imagination, but she thought she saw a flicker of something, as Jacob watched Samuel leave. Something cold. Something hard.

He turned to Mary, his face creasing as he apparently noticed her distress.

"What's wrong?"

"Nothing," said Mary. Lying. She swallowed. "How have you been? Have you managed your irrigation project yet?"

Jacob nodded, still looking as though he wanted to press her for details. But she smiled encouragingly, and he began explaining the work he had done on his and his neighbor's fields.

"It worked so well that I did end up burning some of the wheat so I could plant other things there," he said, leaning his forearms along the top of the gate and craning his head forward to see past the windmill to their right. "Vegetables and so on, things that can grow in the fall."

"Was that this week? I wondered what the smoke was," said Mary.

"I did it in sections, keeping it under control, you know," said Jacob. "I remembered your candle demonstration, I didn't want to risk the windmill going up."

He smiled. And Mary felt the warmth of knowing that he had acknowledged her input. That he was showing her he respected her.

And that he wanted respect in return. Why else would he have come to tell her that he had done as she said and helped his neighbors? He had no other reason to come over.

Mary found herself smiling back. She knew, now, after this evening, that she could never be with Samuel. And when that was done, then who knew? Maybe Jacob...

"Do you know what was wrong with Samuel?" Jacob was asking.

"We just... had a disagreement," said Mary carefully, leaning against the gatepost and looking out at the darkening sky. "Things are a little strained."

"Right..." Jacob glanced toward the house. "Is that..." he stopped.

"Is that what?" asked Mary.

"I was wondering. Um..."

Mary began to feel worried. Jacob was not meeting her eyes. "What is it? Tell me."

"I don't want to overstep," he said, still looking away. "I thought maybe your father had already cleared everything up, when I saw you with Samuel. But then, if you're unhappy about it all – "

"What all?" asked Mary. He was not making any sense.

He looked up, then. Surprised.

"The... you know, about Samuel?" he coughed. "Your brothers were asking around, and one of the men – you know, Eli Miller, he said he had heard a rumor a while back, and he didn't want to spread it but if they were worried..." he trailed off.

Mary was still staring.

"They told your father," he said. "A few days ago. Did he not tell you?"

"No." Mary stepped toward Jacob so she could look him right in the eye, through the settling darkness. "Tell me."

Jacob swallowed. And he told her.

And Mary felt her insides turn to ice.

***

"You don't understand."

"Obviously not," said Mary, her throat tight. "I'm asking you to explain it to me."

They all looked upset. Her father, Paul, Albert. No, not even upset – annoyed. Annoyed that Mary had called them from their work and was pestering them with questions when they had better things to do.

"If there had been any substance to that rumor," her father said through gritted teeth, glancing out through the front window, "of course we would have told you. But we saw no reason to upset you with something that might just be lies."

"But it might have been true," hissed Mary.

Outside, the sky was low and gray, the cloud from the evening before having been joined by a mass of others. There had been no rain, but there was a warm wind gusting hard across the fields, whipping the grass into long, snaking waves.

The men her father had helping him put the grain through the mill would be working frantically to keep up the pace, Mary thought. And her father and brothers obviously wanted to join them. But they had not gone yet. And she knew – she knew, somehow – that this meant they had been caught out. If they truly believed there was nothing to worry about then they would have gone back out to work.

"But that girl wasn't pregnant," Albert pointed out, his mouth twisting distastefully as he said the words. "Obviously."

"She might have lost it," Paul said quietly, though the other two glared at him for this.

"Whether she was or not," said Mary, "the fact that there was reason to think she might have been speaks for itself."

"She might have been lying," said her father.

"Why on earth would she lie about that?" Mary snapped, just managing to stop herself from shouting the words.

She glanced at the door, wishing she had waited for her mother to return from the Yoders' before starting this conversation. Surely she would have understood. But then, would she not have been told the story along with her father? Would she not also have chosen to ignore it?

A low rumble of thunder shook the house. Mary felt herself anticipating the tapping of raindrops on the windowpanes, but none followed. Just more dry wind, more waiting, more frustration.

"We don't know any of these people, from Samuel's old community," her father pointed out. In his calm, collected manner. "We had no reason to think badly of Samuel. Why would we believe such a rumor without proof?"

"I believe it," Mary said.

That, finally, got her father's full attention. Her brothers also looked away from the frantically turning windmill, their expressions matched in horror.

"Mary – you didn't – you and Samuel – "

"What? No," Mary said, shocked in her turn. "*No.*"

"Then why would you – "

"It wasn't – I mean, there were moments." Mary closed her eyes briefly. "When I could tell. If I had let him, he would have."

It had not just been that touch, last night.

It had been in the way he looked at her. His eyes raking her up and down, stopping where they should not. The way he had sought her away from everyone else, the way he blocked her when there were other people present. The way he treated her as though she were already his.

She had chosen not to notice. She had not wanted to.

"How could you not tell me?" she asked quietly.

And then, because if she was ever going to feel justified in asking this question, it was now:

"Was it because of the money?"

And her father would not look at her.

"Was it worth it?" she asked, her voice almost a whisper.

"The windmill," she heard Albert say.

She covered her face with her hands. "Stop it."

"No, the windmill – "

"*I don't care about the – *"

"No, look!"

Albert was pointing, frozen, his face the color of ash. Pointing outside. Across the yard, and the pasture beyond, to the windmill. To the men running away from it. To the thin, dark stream of smoke rising above.

***

"I wondered where you were."

Mary looked up, shielding her eyes, even though the sky was still purpled with clouds. They were still irritated from the smoke, as were the insides of her nose and throat, and she did not want to open them at all. But she managed to smile at Jacob, who looked even worse than she did. He sat down next to her and took off his shoes as she had, joining her as she dangled her feet in the stream. His stream.

He had come running, yesterday. She had seen him from the back pasture, where she had run to with her family once they had realized that they would not be able to put the fire out. Paul and Albert had had to forcibly drag their father away to stop him from trying to get back and save his beloved windmill.

They had run until they heard the explosion of flames behind them which signaled that the flour-filled air inside of the mill had caught. Mary had glimpsed it from the corner of her eye as she had looked behind her; a sudden rush and roar of brightness leaping into the sky.

They had watched as the structure had been eaten away, blackening and crumbling. The fire had spread to the sailcloths, which continued to whip themselves around in the wind, billowing flames and smoke in their wake, flinging burning debris as far as it would go. Onto the dry grass of the next pasture. Into what was left of the wheat fields. Onto the house.

And Jacob had come running, sprinting toward the fire. Dragging them back with him, as the fire and smoke followed them across the dry fields. Back to his home. The only safe place – because, as he had told Mary, he had, just that week, burned a large strip of his land to prepare it for planting. And fire will not burn across something that has been burned already.

Mary's mother had met them as they arrived, her eyes wild with fear. They had stayed standing outside the house, catching their breath, coughing, watching in the distance as everything they owned turned to ash, praying for the rain to start. But the clouds had remained obstinate and aloof, and the fire had continued its path until it petered out at the edges of the wheat fields.

"Have they found out what caused it yet?" Mary asked now.

Jacob shrugged, and covered a cough. He and the others had used the water from his spring to dampen the ground around his house, just in case, and he had had to spend a lot of time in the way of the wind-driven smoke. His skin still looked a little gray, and Mary could smell that he was several baths away from ridding himself of the odor.

"Might have been lightning," he said. "Or the speed of the wind. If there was a piece in the mechanism that hadn't been properly oiled, it could have sparked."

Mary nodded. "To be honest," she said, "I don't really care. And – and I'm glad its gone."

She wondered if she would have to explain herself, but Jacob was nodding. Someone – probably Paul, she thought – had filled him in. On everything.

"I'm sorry for your family's losses," he said, "but honestly – me too."

They paddled their feet for another minute. The air was finally beginning to clear. Somewhere overhead, a bird began to sing, as though assuring the world it remained unmoved by present circumstances.

"Are you leaving with the others?" Jacob asked.

This morning, there had been an emergency meeting called. All the families. There had been talk already of leaving, of heading back to Lancaster. There was no blessing here, some had said. Even if there was rain, now, it would be such hard work to keep going. It was too much. They were ready to leave.

Others had wanted to stay. Jacob's fields had been saved, as had the Kauffman's. A few other families seemed on the fence, each seeming to want someone else to make a firm commitment before they followed. There were five in all. Not that many. But enough for a start.

Mary looked down at her hands, twisted in her lap. "My family want to go," she said.

"I don't blame them," said Jacob. "But do you?"

"How could I stay without them?" asked Mary quietly.

Jacob was silent for a minute.

"You know what I would suggest – what I would ask," he said.

Mary did not reply. She knew. Hers had been the first name he had called, as he had run to them the day before. Hers had been the hand he had held, pulling her to safety. She was the one he had come to, over the course of the afternoon, to check on. To reassure.

There was no hiding it now.

"I know that, after everything, you may have trouble..." Jacob paused. "Trusting."

Mary leaned back, taking her weight on her hands, feeling the dry grass beneath them. She nodded, as though only to herself. Jacob looked at her, his expression indescribably sad.

"I'm so sorry," he said. "About everything. Everything you've been through. But I hope – I have to hope, and I have to ask now, while I can – "

The bird stopped singing.

"Do you trust me?" he asked. "Could you... trust me?"

Mary closed her eyes. She thought about her father. Her brothers. Samuel. The men who she had trusted before.

And then she thought of Jacob. Showing her such care and kindness even when he thought they she could never be his.

And, on her smoke-singed, upturned face, she felt it. The first fat, wet raindrop, hitting her so hard she could hear it against her skin. And another. And another.

The bird flew off, presumably excited about the prospect of worms. And Mary and Jacob stayed where they were. The rain fell harder, and Mary blinked drops off her eyelashes. She caught Jacob looking at her. And smiled.

"Yes," she said. "I do."

MY CHRISTIAN COWBOY

JENNIFER ANN RAMSEY

Chapter One: The Meeting

Bill sat on the porch of his mother's small farm home shining his boots. Bill took pride of his things, and these boots had to last him for the whole season. It was hard to keep boots clean in his line of work.

Bill grew up with his mother in a small town in Missouri. She had lived there since Bill was born over twenty-two years ago. His job took him out west, though. He was a bounty hunter. When someone would break the law, he would go after them and pick them up. When he brought the criminal to the sheriff, he would get a reward. The land wasn't very developed, and most criminals decided to hide out west. Bill worked especially hard to get the job done, which helped develop quite the reputation. Bill needed to catch every criminal he could to get paid. After his father died, his mother was left alone. Bill felt the need to support her. Bill's mother, Annie, didn't exactly like her son's career, but she had to admit that he was good at it.

Annie was starting to wear the wisdom and pain of old age. Her hair was more gray than blonde, and she had wrinkles under her eyes. She was usually seen smiling, though, especially when her son was safe and at home with her. She was known around the small town for her feisty attitude, her cooking, and her talent for making clothes.

"Finish up and come get some of this chili, boy," Annie called out to her son.

"I'm almost done, ma!"

"Well, I don't want to hear a word when your chili is cold."

"Is there cornbread?"

"You ungrateful boy, you better get in here and take what you're given before you get nothing!"

Bill put down his polish and boots and headed into the wooden home. The home was small, but it had a comfortable feeling about it. On the table, next to the kitchen, were two bowls of chili (and cornbread).

"This looks great, ma!" Bill said, sitting down on the bench.

"You are not thinking of having supper before washing up, are you?"

"I'm fine, ma! All I did was go out into town today and get shoe polish."

"You will not sit at my table without washing up. Wash your hands and your face."

Bill obeyed. He spent his days chasing dangerous criminals around the country, but he was still afraid of his mother's whippings.

"So, how long are you staying this time?"

Bill always hated this question. She made him feel guilty, but he had to leave to bring money home. "Sheriff Lawrence told me that he has a job for me. I'm planning on heading there in the morning."

"But you just came home yesterday!"

"I know. I gotta get more money when I can, though. You hardly have any flour left. You have no sugar. I'm glad I came home when I did., but the money that I brought home will only last for so long."

"You know I worry about you when you're not here."

"Just keep busy with church and cooking and your dresses. You won't even know I was gone."

"You know I worry."

Bill saved his cornbread for last. He dipped it in the remainder of the chili in his bowl and took a big bite. "I am gonna miss your cornbread."

After dinner, Annie did the dishes and read the Bible before bed while Bill finished polishing his boots and drank some of his moonshine.

The sun woke Bill up the next morning bright and early. Annie was already up doing her daily chores. Bill went out to feed his horse, Bonnie, and get ready for his next job.

"I suppose I'll see you again in another month or so."

"That depends on how long the job takes me, ma."

"Well, I love you. Be good. I packed you some food to take with you."

With that, Bill got ready for his next job. He rode down to the sheriff's station, and he tied Bonnie up before getting inside. Sheriff O'Malley was a beast of a man. His large stature alone helped to keep order in the area. He also had a large gun that helped.

"Well, there's the top bounty hunter in the whole West looking for another bounty I reckon."

"Well, I need to keep my ma in those nice dress that she makes."

"You know, I've been meaning to tell the wife that it's about time for her to get another Sunday dress. Between you and me, hers is starting to look a little ragged."

"I'm surprised you're willing to spend the money."

"Lord knows I don't want to."

"Well, what have you got for me, Sheriff?"

"To be honest, you've been rounding them up pretty good. We don't have too much right now."

"Come on. You know I gotta work."

"Well, there is one thing, but I'm not sure you'll take it. The Thompsons down in Independence were asking for some help with their daughter. Apparently, they haven't seen her in some time. They will be willing to pay you. They have some money."

"I guess if that's what I need to do then that's what I need to do. I'll head that way right now."

Independence was a bit of a distance, but Bill was sure that she could get there before dinner. He rode throughout the day, only to stop for water a couple of times. When he got to Independence, he stopped at the general store to get some whiskey and some candies. He was also able to ask the person behind the counter to tell him how to get to the Thompson home. He learned that Mr. Thompson was the local pastor, and t he house was just up the road about half a mile.

As Bill came up to the gorgeous but modest house with blue shutters and horses in the back, he saw another site that caught his eye: a young woman in a simple skirt, blouse, and boots. Her hair was in a long, messy braid, and she had the most beautiful smile that Bill had ever seen.

Chapter Two: Katy Thompson and Family

"Excuse me, ma'am. Can you tell me if this is the Thompson residence?"

"I sure can. Katy Thompson. Pleasure to meet you. What brings you around? I haven't seen you here before." The girl spoke with elegance and had a flair of sophistication to her demeanor. Her clothes didn't look especially fancy, but it wasn't Sunday. She also smelled of horses and flowers.

"I'm a bounty hunter and Sheriff O'Malley sent me. I understand that you may need some assistance finding someone.

Katy's eyes lit up. "Oh, come this way. My folks will be so happy to see you. They have been worried sick. Here, let your horse in back with the others. She's not too mean, is she? I don't want her scaring my horse."

"Nope. She's a gentle giant. She'll be just fine."

Katy was moving quickly. "I am so happy that you're here!"

Bill followed the beautiful girl into the family home. The house smelled like cherry pie, and Bill was suddenly painfully aware of how hungry he was.

"Mama! Papa! This man here says he wants to help find Lizzie."

The small family gathered into the main room quickly. Bill could feel the hope in the air the way that the family was so excited.

"Please! Come in. What's your name?"

"Do you know where Lizzie is?

"Are you hungry? Can I get you something to eat? Take off your boots. You're our guest."

When they finally stopped talking, Bill sat down and slowly took off his boots. He could feel the eyes on him.

"My name is Bill. I'm a bounty hunter by trade, and my local sheriff said that you were looking for help. I'm his number one bounty hunter, and I have a very good success rate."

"She's not a criminal or anything," Mr. Thompson said quickly. "She's just always been a little wild. She was always a good girl. She would help me at church every Sunday. It wasn't until recently that she started misbehaving."

"What was she doing to misbehave?"

"Well, she started dating a boy. I told her that I disapproved, but she wasn't going to let that stop her. I often wish that I had just let her date him. Maybe she would still be with us if I had," said Mrs. Thompson.

"Don't blame yourself, mama."

"And you guys have no idea where she might have gone?" Bill asked.

"She probably left with her boyfriend to Shadow Creek. The only problem is that it is quite far away in Kansas," said Katy. "Her boyfriend had family there."

"I simply can't abandon my congregation. They need me."

Bill nodded. "Well, I am happy to go travel down there and bring her back for you. That's no problem."

"Oh, thank you! We will pay you. We will pay you everything that we have. We just want our little girl back," said Mrs. Thompson.

"I will only need a couple of supplies and a small advance. When I return with Lizzie, we can complete the payment," said Bill. "I'll leave tomorrow. Now, as the first part of the payment, do you think that I can have some of whatever smells so darn delicious around here?"

"Yes! Yes! Yes! Katy, go whip him up a plate."

"Absolutely, mama."

"We will have to send the sheriff our thanks for sending you to us. You are the answer to our prayers," said Mr. Thompson.

"Well," said Bill," I appreciate it, but don't thank me too much yet. You can thank me when I come back with your daughter. And maybe I can enjoy one of your sermons then."

"Oh, that would be wonderful. You will be my special guest," said Mr. Thompson.

"What happens if she says she doesn't want to come back?" Katy asked putting a plate in front of Bill. "I mean, why would she just leave with some stranger?"

"I can be very convincing," said Bill. "It's my job to take people where they don't want to go. This will not be new for me."

"You're not going to hurt her, are you?" asked Mrs. Thompson.

"I generally don't even have to hurt the fugitives that I bring in. I don't think that a little woman will be too difficult," said Bill. "The boyfriend might catch a beating, though. It depends on what I find."

Mr. Thompson got a serious look on his face. "Now, I can't condone violence, Mr. Bill. Jesus taught us to turn the other cheek, and I have to maintain that sentiment. However, I would not be upset if you didn't bring him back with you."

"And what's so bad about him?" Bill asked.

"He lives an immoral life. He drinks He gambles. He was exciting, but Lizzie doesn't need excitement. She needs to be at home with her family. She needs to be a respectable girl," said Mrs. Thompson. "It's not acceptable for her to be running off like this."

"And how old is Lizzie?" Bill asked.

"Sixteen-years-old. Almost two years under me," said Katy.

"Well, thank you all so much for the meal and the hospitality. I think that I should be heading to sleep as soon as possible. I want to be sure to leave early in the morning."

"Absolutely. You can sleep in Lizzie's bed for the night. It's next to Katy's. Katy will sleep with us in our room tonight. She can show you where your bed is."

Katy showed Bill the small bed in a small room in the house. "It's not much, but it will do," Katy said giving him pillows.

The next morning, Mrs. Thompson had a nice sack of food and other supplies. As he was getting ready to head out, he saw Katy running in from doing her chores.

"Mama! Wait!"

"What is it, child?"

"Mama, I want to go with."

Chapter Three: A Travel Companion

"You can't be serious," Mrs. Thompson said.

"Mama, please. I know she'll come home if I go with," said Katy.

"And who do you suppose is going to do your chores while you're gone?" asked Mrs. Thompson.

"Mama, I haven't gone anywhere in my whole life. Lizzie just ran off. I just want to go with to get her. To see something new," said Katy.

"I'm not having my second daughter run away too," said Mr. Thompson walking out the front door. "I say we let her go. There's only one problem, Katy."

"What's that, pa?"

"The decision isn't really up to us. You'd be a burden on Bill here. Now, that's not really fair to him is it?"

Bill didn't know how to respond. The girl would be a complete burden. She would slow him down, and she would use up his rations. He would have to protect her the whole time, too. "It can get pretty dangerous out there, little lady. I ride fast, too."

"I can ride faster!" she said quickly. "I've been riding these guys since I was young. I am the fastest "rider in town."

"I'll have to spend my time looking after you. I don't want to see you get hurt."

"I've never fallen off my horse before. I can't imagine that anyone would try to hurt us. It's a simple trip down to Kansas and back. And I will be a help. Not a burden."

Bill scoffed. He didn't care how pretty Katy was, he knew that she was going to be a hassle on this trip. He could also see that she wasn't going to let go.

"Get ready quickly. I'll also need more pay, of course."

"Of course," Mr. Thompson said. "Naturally, you will be properly compensated."

Bill nodded and looked over at Katy who was simply giddy. "Well, hurry up!" he said.

"Oh, yes. Of course!" she said running inside. When she came back out, Bill could already tell that Katy had too much stuff with her.

"Are you sure you want to carry all of that on a ride all the way to Kansas?"

"I'll be just fine," Katy said stubbornly as she started loading up her horse.

"Just don't come whining to me when the load is too heavy for you."

"Jeez. I said that I got it, didn't I?"

Bill could start to see exactly how this trip was going to go. As they started riding, though, he was pleasantly surprised at how well she could ride. He stayed behind her to make sure that he could keep an eye on her, and she maintained a decent speed the whole time. She didn't even complain much. Bill was worried that she would need to stop for a break every hour. She went a good six hours before even suggesting stopping for a drink of water. Her face was sweaty, and she was clearly very thirsty- she drank quite a bit. It made Bill giggle internally because he knew that she had gone as far as she possibly could before stopping to show him how tough she was. He decided to make a point to suggest small stops for water more often.

"We're gonna ride until sundown and then set up camp," Bill said. "Eat a small bite now, but we'll eat when we're settled."

"Are we going to find a store?"

"We have food. There's no need for that."

"I thought that we just had some bread and some preserves."

"Hopefully, I can catch a rabbit or something. We can have some meat."

Katy didn't complain. They just went ahead and continued riding for the four hours that they had planned. It was just after sun dark, and they found a quiet area to set up camp off of the road.

"We didn't do so bad for the first day. We'll probably get there in another two or three days," Bill said as he built the fire.

"I really do thank you for bringing me along," Katy said.

"Yeah. Just try to keep up the same pace as today, and you won't be too much of an inconvenience," Bill said.

When the fire was burning, he pulled out a small flask of whiskey from his jacket.

"Are you going to drink on this trip?" Katy said, sounding amazed.

"Ma'am, I am bringing you along on my trip. I would ask you to be so kind as to not tell me what I can and cannot do."

Katy went silent.

"So your sister- is she in love with the guy?" Bill finally said.

"I'm sorry?" she asked.

"The guy that your sister ran off with- is she in love with him?"

"I suppose that she thinks that she is. I don't know about if they're actually in love, though. I hope not. That will make this whole ordeal a hell of a lot harder."

"If they are in love, don't you think that they should stay together?"

"I guess we'll have to talk to her about that when we get to Shadow Creek."

The two then turned silent again for some time. Bill wasn't used to having women with him on his trips, and he was happy that Katy wasn't too chatty. He didn't mind the company, though.

"You know I've never been this far out before. It's absolutely beautiful," Katy said. "It's like seeing the world through different eyes. I'm in a different state doing a different job. You get to travel like this all the time?"

"Yep," said Bill.

"You know, I think they have more stars here than in Independence. Or the stars seem brighter. Something just makes them better here."

"Yep," said Bill. He took another swig out of his flask.

"Does that make you fall over? There was this boy in my school, Johnny. He found his daddy's liquor and started drinking it. He fell over in front of everybody. His daddy beat him so badly that he had to sit on a cushion the next day."

"I can handle my liquor," Bill said.

"Well, I think I'm going to head to bed. I might try to count the stars. Thank you again, Mr. Bill." Katy walked up to him and gave him a big hug. It startled Bill at first, but he went ahead and hugged her back. He didn't know how she did it, but she still smelled like horses and flowers.

"Goodnight."

Chapter Four: Beauty

"Watch where you're going!"Bill called out. Katy was going dangerously fast, laughing the whole time. In fact, she was almost going faster than Bill could manage. She seemed to have a true bond with the horse, and they moved as one. They would lean in the same direction and they both seemed to know when they were going to go for a small jump or go around an object.

"I can go slower if it's too fast for you!" the laughing girl called back.

"It's not too fast for me. I'm supposed to keep you safe. I don't need you falling."

"What? I can't hear you. You're getting pretty far behind, Mr. Bill!"

Bill kicked Bonnie to make her go faster, but the horse was going as fast as she could go. Bill kicked Bonnie again, and she got up on her hind legs, neighing. Bill felt a sharp pain as he fell on the dirt ground. He could see the blood scattered in front of him.

He heard Katy running toward him. Once again, she was laughing. "Seriously, if it was too fast for you, you should have said something. I would have slowed down."

Bill was finally able to get up, but he was still feeling some pain.

"I'm not the one who couldn't go faster. It was Bonnie who couldn't go faster. She's getting old."

"Here, let me help you clean up. Let's go back to that stream we passed."

Bill got back on Bonnie (after apologizing for kicking her) and they gently trotted over to the stream.

"Come here. I have a rag," said Katy. As she stood in front of his with the damp cloth,cleaning his wounds, she was amazingly gentle. When she blew softly on the wound, Bill could see that her eyes were the prettiest color of brown that he had ever seen. She maintained a smile the entire time.

"There. You're all better," Katy said. "You want to sit for a minute?"

"Desperately," Bill said. "I'm also starving."

"Well, we can have these biscuits." Katy handed him some biscuits that she had in a napkin in her pocket.

"Are you eating while riding?"

"I try," Katy laughed. "But mostly I keep them to have them ready for Thunder over there. My mama says I spoil him, but he's always been my favorite."

"You are a very good rider."

"It's my favorite thing in the whole wide world. It makes me feel at one with nature. At one with God. I'd kinda lost that feeling lately, but this trip really helped make me remember how much I love riding Thunder."

"Bonnie's been with me since I was young. It was my first horse, and I took care of her more than I took care of myself. I'd be dirty, but she'd be spotless," Bill said.

"How old is she?"

"She is almost fifteen years old," Bill said. "I'm planning on leaving her with my mom and getting a young stud, but I just can't bare to part with her."

"You'll still see her all of the time," said Katy. "Well, is it time to get back to it? We have a long way to go still."

"Yeah," Bill said. "Let's get going."

They rode at the same pace as the day before and continued through the wilderness. The further they got, the more distracted Katy got by the sites.

"Are those buffalo? Look! I think that there are buffalo down there."

"The town has an entire shop just for ice cream?"

Bill knew that he had to focus on the job at hand, so he kept the mesmerized girl on track. They didn't stop once, although he secretly wanted to show her the sights as much as she wanted to see them. He never wanted to do that before. Could this girl be having an effect on him?

They continued traveling until sundown. Their routine was very similar to their routine the night before. They set up camp off of the road, Bill created a fire, and they had dinner by the fire. Bill noticed that Katy was a little closer to him than she was the night before.

"Tell me about yourself, Bill."

"What's there to tell? I grew up in St. Louis. My dad was gone when I was little. I work to help take care of my ma and my horses."

"Do you have a wife?"

"Nope."

"Do you ever want a wife?"

"I never thought about it before."

"Have you ever kissed a woman?"

"Plenty of times."

"You scoundrel!"

"Not at all. It just never works out."

"Do you like your job?"

"Yep."

"Are you ever lonely?"

"Not really. No."

"Do you think that I'm pretty?"

"Yep. You look fine."

They both went back to eating until they finished their dinner. Katy immediately got up to clean the supplies before bed. Bill sat back and sipped on his whiskey until she came back.

"'The stars are amazing again tonight."

"I reckon they are."

"How many stars do you think there are?"

"Millions. Maybe more."

"I'm just going to lay here and watch the stars."

"That sounds nice."

Katy laid down on the ground next to Bill. She gently laid her head against his shoulder. They sat in silence, and she stared at the stars. Bill hoped that she couldn't feel his heart beating a little more quickly than normal while she was so close. They laid there together for a good twenty minutes.

"I think I'm going to head to bed now," Katy said. And she got up and kissed Bill softly. Bill was shocked but received her kiss tenderly. Her lips were the softest that he had ever felt. "Goodnight."

Chapter Five: A Gift

"Let's get going!" called out Bill. "If we hurry up, we will be able to get there tonight."

"You really think so?" asked Katy.

"It's a stretch but maybe. If not, we'll be very close. We can get there early tomorrow."

"This wasn't so bad!"

"This wasn't that far of a ride. Trust me, it can be quite grueling."

"I believe you! I am starting to feel it in my legs."

They continued to ride through the countryside together only stopping for water and short breaks. Bill started to get excited for even those short times with the beautiful girl. She was pretty, she was funny, and she was tough. Most importantly, he hadn't felt quite so alive as he did on this trip with her. He felt privileged to even be able to drink water next to her. He wasn't sure how to interpret the kiss from the night before. They had not talked about the kiss at all, and it was the only thing that Bill could think about.

It was still light when they got to a small town.

"Hey, let's stop here for awhile," Bill said.

"Can we get some candy maybe?" asked Katy.

"We might be able to do that."

They tied up their horses and started walking around the small town. People were outside, and it was a gorgeous night out. Katy's hair was in her usual long braid that always had some wild strands framing her face.

"So were you just tired?" Katy asked.

"Naw. I saw this little town and thought we might enjoy some civilization."

"Well, you have me with you!"

"And you're wonderful company. I also wouldn't mind some candy, though."

"Look! There's the general store. I'm sure my folks will give you an extra couple of dollars for anything you buy me on the trip."

"I'm not worried about it," Bill said.

The general store was larger than most small town general stores. It had a large selection of everything from food, cigarettes, tools, animal feed, crafts, Bibles, clothing, and jewelry.

"Look at that Bible! It's absolutely beautiful!" said Katy. She ran to an ornate Bible with bold colors and fantastic pictures. Katy flipped through the Bible excitedly. This is the most beautiful thing that I had ever seen!"

"It's quite stunning."

"I wonder how much it is."

"More than we have," Bill said. "It sure is nice, though. They have a lot of nice things at this store."

"I know! Look at that bracelet. That looks like real silver. Do you think that there's real silver in there?"

"I think so. And it looks like there is turquoise, too."

"It's the most beautiful thing that I had ever seen. Oh, the other girls in town would be so jealous if they saw me wearing this. This is better than most wedding rings."

"Let's get back to the candy."

Bill and Katy looked through the numerous cartons of candies and picked out a couple of bags full to take with them. Bill also went ahead and bought a coca cola for them to share outside before riding more.

"Well, we should probably get headed out," Bill said.

"Yep. I'm glad that you suggested stopping here, though."

"Go get the horses ready and I'll be right there, OK?"

"Yes, sir."

Bill waited until Katy was out of view before going into the store to buy the silver bracelet and the Bible.

They rode on until they couldn't see anymore and set up camp.

"Are we close?" asked Katy.

"We'll make it by tomorrow."

"Great. I'm so excited to see my sister."

"She'll be happy to see you, too. I think it will definitely help in getting her to come home."

"I hope that she's not with that good for nothing man of hers anymore."

"Did you save her any pieces of candy?" Bill asked.

Katy had her last piece of candy in her hand and threw it into her mouth and shrugged. "I came all the way out here to come get her. Not bring her candy."

After they had a small dinner, Katy took care of their supplies again. She was very good at keeping things clean. When she got back, she immediately sat very close to Bill and put his arm around her.

"I like watching the stars with you," Bill said.

Katy shushed him and continued looking up into the sky. While she sat with his arm around her, she linked fingers with him. Bill loved the feel of her soft, small fingers in between his.

After a couple of minutes, Bill took her face in his hands and brought her in for their second kiss. She leaned in for more, but Bill leaned back.

"I got you something," he said .

"You have more candy?"

"I think you might like it a little more than that." Bill went into his pocket and pulled out the silver and turquoise bracelet that Katy had loved so much in the store.

Katy's eyes lit up. "It can't be! Bill, I- I love it. Oh, but we have to take it back. My parents will never let me have it. It costs too much. They can't pay you back."

"No. This is from me. I want you to have it."

"Are you sure?"

"I'm very sure."

Katy started to tear up, and she immediately took the bracelet and put it on. "It's the most beautiful thing in the whole wide world!" she screamed. She then wrapped her arms around Bill's neck and passionately kissed him.

"You can't wear it while you're riding," Bill said.

"I know."

"It's for church and when you have company over and all."

"OK"

"And you have to clean it once a month."

"Oh, please just kiss me."

Chapter Six: Lizzie Thompson

The sun lit Katy up like an angel. Bill had woken up early to get to Shadow Creek as soon as possible, and Katy was still sleeping in her blankets.

"Good morning!"

Katy woke up in a bit of a daze.

"It's not even light out yet."

"We're getting an early start. We don't want to get to your sister any later than we have to."

Katy and Bill were on the trail before anyone else that morning. They traveled with purpose, and they traveled quickly.

"How long do you think that it will take us?" Katy asked.

"It will probably be about four hours. Maybe six. I'm hoping that we get there by noon."

At their first stop to let the horses drink water, Bill couldn't help but cuddle with Katy on the river bank.

They continued riding throughout the morning enjoying the breeze hitting their face and continually exchanged jokes throughout the ride. They even raced a little bit across one clear meadow.

"We're coming up to Shadow Creek!" Bill screamed.

"We are?"

"Yep! We'll be with your sister soon enough!"

Bill was right- they rode up to the town shortly after. It was another small town. It wouldn't be too hard to find Lizzie.

"Can I put my bracelet on while we're in town?"

"Don't be silly. It's for Sunday and special occasions. You'll wear it to church the next time you go."

"Well, I'm showing Lizzie. Now, how do we find her?"

"Let's start by asking at the general store. Everybody in town has to shop there."

The couple went into the store and Katy immediately started running.

"Lizzie!" she screamed. Lizzie was there at the general store. It was the perfect timing.

Bill watched the two girls embrace before introducing him.

"Hi, Lizzie. I'm Bill. I came down here with Katy to get you."

"I'll tell you everything after I'm done scolding her for running off in the first place. What were you thinking? What about ma and pa?"

"I'm so sorry, Katy. And I'm so glad that you're here. He's awful. He's absolutely awful."

"What did he do to you, Lizzie? Does he beat you?"

"Once. He drinks and yells a lot, though. I made a horrible mistake. I need to go home."

"Well, mama and papa are going to be happy to have you back. But we gotta go tell him that you're leaving."

"He's gone for the day. I don't want to wait to tell him. I just want to take the horse and go now. I'll leave a note."

Bill, Katy, and Lizzie went back to Lizzie's small home to leave a note for the man that she was leaving. Bill didn't want to get too involved, but he was secretly very happy that he could bring Lizzie back to her family and away from the abusive boyfriend. He was also just happy to see how relieved Katy was.

It didn't take long for the three to start to head back to Independence. The girls spent a good portion of the first day of the trip talking in secret. Bill could only assume that it was girl talk about him. When they set up camp for the night, he immediately put his arm around Katy in front of her sister.

Lizzie started teasing them and asked desperately to see the bracelet that Katy had been going on about. He brought out the bracelet and started realizing that he could truly enjoy a life with Katy. There was only one very important thing to do first.

They made it back in four days. The sun was going down, but no one wanted to camp another night. They pushed through until they finally saw the small gorgeous house with the blue shutters. Bill followed the girls as they excitedly put their horses away and got ready to surprise their parents.

Mr and Mrs. Thompson were in the main room by the fire when they walked in. They had huge smiles and both ran to Lizzie to greet her.

"Oh, honey. Why would you do that to us? I'm so glad that you're home," said Mrs. Thompson, hugging her daughter.

"Lizzie, you have a lot of chores to make up," Mr. Thompson said.

"Let her relax at least for the night," said Mrs. Thompson. "You put your stuff away and clean up and relax tonight. You are going to be worked pretty hard in the morning, though."

"I can't thank you enough for bringing our daughter back home to us," Mr. Thompson told Bill.

"It was truly my pleasure, sir. Your daughters are both amazing people. In fact, Katy and I got really close on the trip-"

"Daddy! Bill bought Katy the prettiest ring I've ever seen! And she said that they kissed!" Lizzie blurted.

Mr. Thompson gave Katy and Bill a suspicious look for a moment. "I assume that you are a good person if you were sent here by Sheriff O'Malley. I look forward to getting to know you while you court my daughter."

Katy looked relieved. "Oh, thank you, daddy. Thank you! Let me show you the bracelet."

"Thank you very much, sir. I really was hoping for your approval. I also got a small present for you as well. I know that you're a man of God, so I thought that it would be a nice addition for either the home or the church," said Bill.

"What are you talking about?" Katy asked.

"I didn't tell you, but I got your dad a gift, too. I wanted to ask for the right to court you properly. I'll be right back."

Bill came back with the elaborate Bible that he and Katy had seen at the General Store. The whole family was in awe, and everyone passed the beautiful book around.

"This will be the nicest Bible at the church," Mr. Thompson said.

"Come on, sweetheart," Katy said. "Let's go look at the stars."

<u>FOR MORE CHRISTIAN ROMANCE</u>[1]

---

1.   http://www.pochepictures.com/christianromance.html